The Frenetic People

The Frenetic People

by
Ernest Pérochon

translated, annotated and introduced by
Brian Stableford

A Black Coat Press Book

ISBN 978-1-61227-118-7. First Printing. November 2012. Published by Black Coat Press, an imprint of Hollywood Comics.com, LLC, P.O. Box 17270, Encino, CA 91416. All rights reserved. Except for review purposes, no part of this book may be reproduced or transmitted in any form or by any means, electronic or mechanical, including photocopying, recording, or by any information storage and retrieval system, without permission in writing from the publisher. The stories and characters depicted in this novel are entirely fictional. Printed in the United States of America.

Introduction

Les Hommes frénétiques by Ernest Pérochon, here translated as *The Frenetic People*, was initially published in Paris by Plon in 1925. It was an anomaly within the author's works, his fame resting almost entirely on his numerous *romans paysans*: stories of rural life focusing primarily on the lives of the poor people who worked the land. He had been producing such fiction since 1912, having been born in 1885 on a farm in Courlay, not far from Parthenay in the département of Deux-Sèvres in western France.

Pérochon had been something of an anomaly himself in that environment; although his own family was not exceedingly poor, his neighbors were, and he later recalled, as a significant memory of his formative childhood, that he had routinely taken off his shoes when he went out to play, lest he be thought effeminate by his barefoot playmates. His own family was Protestant, while most of the neighbors were Catholic—and, indeed, owed allegiance to a particularly militant religious tradition. Having completed his secondary education in Parthenay, Pérochon did not go to university in Paris because he had two younger brothers who still had to complete their secondary studies, and he had to earn a living. He became a schoolteacher, and remained in that profession until 1921, save for his compulsory military service and conscription during the Great War. He married a schoolmistress in 1907; their only child, a daughter, was born the following year.

Pérochon paid for the publication of his first volume of poetry in Niort, the chief town of the département, in 1908, and his first novel, *Les Creux de Maisons*, appeared four years later, initially in serial form in *L'Humanité*, a periodical edited by the socialist propagandist Jean Jaurès. Although Pérochon was mobilized in 1914, he suffered a heart attack at the front and was invalided out of the army. He continued writing, and in 1920 his novel *Néné* won the Prix Goncourt, a success that enabled him to devote himself to writing full-time. His career proceeded smoothly until the invasion of France in Second World War, when his refusal to collaborate with the Vichy government put him in a dangerous situation. His daughter and son-in-law joined the Resistance; the latter escaped from Buchenwald after being captured, and worked for the prosecution at the Nuremberg trials, but Pérochon did not live to see that, having died of a heart attack in 1942.

Inevitably, the effects of the Great War were clearly displayed in the naturalistic novels Pérochon published after 1918, especially in those with which he followed *Néné*, but the most obvious and most striking legacy of the war on his thinking was the production of *Les Hommes frénétiques*, one of a group of apocalyptic fantasies produced in the wake of the war, expressing and explaining the fear that the productions of science were now arming people far too powerfully for their own good, and that future resurgences of belligerence might eventually lead to the annihilation of the race.

Such anxieties were also commonplace in British scientific romance throughout the 1920s and 1930s, producing numerous classics of that genre, including Edward Shanks' *The People of the Ruins* (1920), Cicely Hamilton's *Theodore Savage* (1922; revised as *Lest Ye*

Die), Shaw Desmond's *Ragnarok* (1926), Neil Bell's *The Gas War of 1940* (1931; also known as *Valiant Clay*) and S. Fowler Wright's *Four Days War* (1936) and *Megiddo's Ridge* (1937). The French texts reflecting the same anxiety are, however, generally more extreme—as might be expected, given that France had suffered actual invasion and had provided the theaters for some of the war's most furious fighting and heaviest casualty figures. The French examples are more inclined to push all the way to the horizons of the imagination, often displacing their exemplary conflicts into more remote time-periods of in order that more powerful scientific weaponry could be deployed to more devastating effect.

Notable examples of French apocalyptic fantasies of this stripe published before *Les Hommes frénétiques* included Edmond Haraucourt's "Le Conflit suprême" (1919; tr. as "The Supreme Conflict")[1] and Henri Allorge's *Le Grand cataclysme* (1922; tr. as *The Great Cataclysm*)[2], while José Moselli's *La Fin d'Illa* (1925; tr. as *Illa's End*)[3] was almost exactly contemporary with Pérochon's novel. The last-named is set in the distant past rather than the future, but reflects a notion that became commonplace in fiction of this sort: that previous civilizations had existed on Earth, which had annihilated themselves, and almost all traces of their existence, by means of advanced scientific weaponry; the principal corollary of that notion was that the anticipated demise of humankind might be a phase in a repetitive cycle.

---

[1] Included in the Black Coat Press collection *Illusions of Immortality*, ISBN 978-1-61227-075-3.
[2] Available from Black Coat Press, ISBN 978-1-61227-026-5.
[3] Available from Black Coat Press, ISBN 978-1-61227-031-9.

In terms of the sheer brutality of its excess, Pérochon's novel cannot quite compete with Moselli's, but its far greater sophistication and mock-laconic attention to detail renders its account of superscientific warfare even more effective in its horror. While most of the British scientific romances in this vein are uniquely preoccupied with the destructive effects of poison gases, biological weapons and potential products of atomic disintegration, Pérochon takes all of those easily-foreseeable eventualities in his stride. His physics moves beyond the possibility of providing a theoretical basis for the manufacture crude atomic bombs to a more fundamental examination of the underlying fabric of space, permitting the technological production of exotic forms of matter, energy and—most interestingly—life.

The French *roman scientifique* already had a long tradition of apocalyptic fantasies prior to the Great War, including a particular fascination with the future ruins of Paris, but in those prior fantasies the damage had almost always been done by natural catastrophes, usually major geological upheavals; after the war, such natural catastrophes usually took a back seat, the primary means of destruction being placed firmly in human hands, where they are invariably abused. Pérochon's novel not only takes that notion to an ultimate limit, but offers a more precise account than any of his predecessors of the inexorable logic of that misuse. His account of the particular political opposition that provokes the future war has a deliberately absurd, quasi-satirical component, but it harks back to the fundamental opposition sketched out in 1834 in Félix Bodin's prospectus for *Le Roman de l'avenir* (tr. as *The Novel of the Future*)[4], in which con-

---

[4] Available from Black Coat Press, ISBN 978-1-934543-44-3.

structive political pragmatism is opposed by an "Anti-Prosaic League" of restless (or frenetic) dissidents.

It had been common in futuristic works produced in France prior to the Great War for writers to anticipate the eventual permanent suppression of war by the advent of weapons too dreadful to use, although the killing power assumed to be capable of creating such dread increased dramatically between the 1830s and 1914. In the post-war fantasies, that myth had withered and died; it was taken for granted that the routine escalation of hostilities would inevitably lead to the use of the most powerful weapons available, no matter how dreadful they might be—even at the cost of the extermination of the race—because the desire to destroy the enemy is always mightier the instinct of self-preservation. Although Pérochon was by no means alone in making that assertion in the 1920s, and providing a graphic illustration of it, *Les Hommes frénétiques* deserves to be reckoned as the most dramatic and forceful exemplification of the theme, and thus ranks as a classic of its kind and era. It is not particularly surprising that it is the work of a writer who had no special interest in futuristic fiction as a genre, but had one particular gnawing anxiety that he wanted to express as fully as possible—and once having done so, felt no need to repeat himself or add anything further.

It is probably worth noting, in this context, that the adjective *frénétique* and the associated noun *frénésie* carry wider and subtler implications in French than their English equivalents, "frenetic" or "frantic" and "frenzy." Although Pérochon's *hommes frénétiques* are certainly frenetic in the English sense, in that their quotidian mental restlessness gradually develops into something far worse, their initial plight also harks back to a previous

9

employment of the term in the context of the *fin-de-siècle* Decadent Movement, where it had been associated with a fuller account of the origins and psychopathology of *frénésie*.

The movement in question had taken its cue from Charles Baudelaire's emphatic use of the terms *ennui* and *spleen*, which regarded those acute and aggravated reactions to the conditions of modern society as a spur to both moral decadence and to the literary deployment of "decadent style." Reduced to its simplest form, the thesis suggests that when a society reaches a phase in which its privileged members are ensured not merely of the supply of all their basic needs but also all available luxuries, they will develop new and profoundly unhealthy appetites to replace the ones that have been sated, because many, if not all, humans are constitutionally incapable of contentment and placidity. The writers of the *fin-de-siècle* movement, naturally bent on extrapolation rather than mere repetition, had not been content with Baudelaire's magnification of *ennui* into *spleen*, and had added frénésie to the list as a kind of this phase. The most ambitious attempted summation of the Movement's worldview, produced at the moment of its own terminal decay, Jean Lorrain's *Monsieur de Phocas. Astarté* (1900; tr. as *Monsieur de Phocas*), is one of several texts attempting such a supplementation; the novel's central character is symbolically named the Duc de Fréneuse.

The Decadent Movement was long dead before Ernest Pérochon began writing, and he had not the slightest sympathy with its moral and stylistic contortions, but it had existed and it had made its mark, in terms of the promotion of a psychological thesis that seemed even more plausible in the 1920s, after the Great War, than it had seemed before. Pérochon takes that notion as his departure-point, arguing that no period of peaceful plenty can last long in human affairs, because the absence of the old sources of social stress will inevitably give birth to a stress of its own.

In fact, Pérochon's cynicism cuts even deeper than the cynicism of Decadent fiction; his most challenging suggestion, posed in his first chapter, is that that peace and plenty are only possible, even temporarily, if two of the ideals normally considered virtuous—courage and justice—can be suppressed or set aside. It is, he suggests, the desire for an impossible justice that has always been the primary motive impelling people to slaughter one another mercilessly on a massive scale, and a stupid courage that has always provided them with the psychological means. That supposition makes *Les Hommes frénétiques* distinctive in the tradition of utopian and dystopian literature, posing a moral and pragmatic question in respect to the desirability and practicality of justice (and hence of liberty, equality and fraternity) that most other works of that stripe are content to gloss over. For that reason too, it is an important work within its genre and era, and remains well worth reading today.

Needless to say, the anxieties the novel reflects have not gone away, but have merely been anaesthetized by familiarity.

This translation has been taken from a copy of the 1971 Marabout reprint of *Les Hommes frénétiques*. I have not had an opportunity to compare that edition with the Plon original, but have no reason to think that it is in any way different.

Brian Stableford

THE FRENETIC PEOPLE

PART ONE: HARRISSON THE CREATOR

I. Averine's Century

As seven o'clock was chiming on the nearby meridian, Harrisson appeared on the terrace. After that day, entirely spent in the terrible atmosphere of the subterranean laboratory, the young scientist experienced a keen joy as he breathed in the fresh air laden with inexhaustible vegetal odors.

Having taken off his the outer element of his working clothes—a natural silk smock lined with insulating pellicle—he held the vulgar garment at arm's length momentarily, then pirouetted, and, with a childish gesture suddenly threw it to his right. The smock floated in the air for a second and landed on top of Samuel, a young mulatto, who was crouching down and playing with a kitten.

Harrisson burst out laughing; the cat mewed and Samuel cried out while struggling in the folds of the fabric.

"Damn it, Sam! Now you're trampling on my smock with the thousand glorious stains! Does respect never enter your bird's brain?"

"Bad! Bad!" cried the frightened adolescent. Disentangled from the smock, he retreated, clutching his pet in his arms.

"Bad boy yourself!" Harrisson went on. "When you've torn my ceremonial garment, how can I go abroad in society? What will our great poet Lahorie say, who compares me to a Beast of the Apocalypse? What will the Academies say...?"

He was speaking in a loud and joyful voice. Suddenly, he fell silent and stood still, seemingly confused.

Then, in the silence that had fallen, a soft and serious voice was heard: "Play, my sons!"

Harrisson advanced to the front of the terrace, where an old man was reclining in an old-style armchair. "Master," he murmured, "I'm sorry for having interrupted your nap with these noisy and stupid capers."

A powerful white-haired head detached itself from the high back of the chair: a fine patriarchal head with eyes of infinite softness.

"Play, youngsters! You, grown-up Luc, with your head full of light, and you, little Samuel with the sparkling laugh, play without constraint. The sight of your gaiety is soothing to my feeble eyes."

"But you were asleep, Master, and we woke you up!"

"I was asleep? And you woke me up? I'm not sure about that. For me, there's no longer anything but uncertainty... Sleep...life...death...it all gets mixed up, But gaiety is a sure and good thing. I understand your gaiety. I like your gaiety."

The voice became softer still, more veiled and more distant. "I believe I thought...yes, thought clearly...during my long, prideful life...a hundred years long, soon! A hundred years, flowing by like a stream...like the wind. I said: this is true; that is false! Here's the just, and the unjust! I weighed the exact measure, with harsh honesty…but my soul no longer distinguishes reliably between light and shadow…my mind is pale and smooth…here's the evening, miraculous and soft…here's the dream!"

The old man closed his eyes again.

Already, Samuel had resumed playing with his pet. He had not been listening. He was a curiously backward child, but without any morbid symptoms; expert psychologists saw him, not as ill, but as a specimen of Neolithic humankind. In his obscure brain, the simplest words only awoke fugitive images. Perfectly beautiful, the natural harmony of his gestures was a joy to watch. When he was resting, Harrisson let him play nearby. This evening, however, annoyed by his routines, he sent him away.

Samuel, who liked the scientist's presence, pleaded with him.

With a gesture, Harrisson showed him the door. "Go!"

The child drew away sadly, his cat in his arms.

The old man seemed to be asleep. In spite of the approach of dusk, it was still warm. Sure of not being disturbed, Harrisson took off his tunic with a sigh of discouragement. Then he took off the thin insulating pellicle that protected his arms and wrists.

For a month, he had been living in his private laboratory, spending all day and part of the night there. He lived there alone, because of the infernal atmosphere, to which the assistants could not accustom themselves, and, most of all, because of the unknown dangers. Against ordinary dangers, of course, all precautions had been taken. Harrisson did not fear those dangers; he had proved to himself the impossibility of presently-explicable accidents—but it was necessary to anticipate considerable and terrible surprises. The domain that the young scientist was exploring, the extravagant domain of the imponderable, was inconceivably various, and, in spite of numerous endeavors, it still remained a fearful novelty.

Harrisson likened himself to some adventurous pioneer of primitive eras, leaving the horde to penetrate alone, always further forward, into the mystery of an unknown forest. The forest was limitless, populated by unimaginable forms, and possessed of a mobility such that the fugitive images of an absurd dream would have seemed stable, clear and admissible by comparison: a realm of madness, full of an immense confusion of chimeras.

Madness! Scientists of previous centuries, and even of today, thinkers overly accustomed to the old rules, might perhaps have felt the wind in their face—but he, Harrisson, was untroubled as he watched idols totter and theories collapse that had formed the foundations of human mentality for centuries. He observed, measured, counted; he noted alarming results, and shrugged his shoulders whenever a philosopher, speaking from the height of his ignorance, accused him of merely rejuvenating old utopias and propagating elementary absurdities.

A virile joy swelled his breast; once again, his research was about to reach a conclusion: not a definitive result, such as only exists in the minds of poets and the ignorant, but a result that would count for something nevertheless in the history of human trial and error.

Thanks to him, a new combination of forces had come into play. He had just done something that no human had ever done before. For a brief moment, at a singular point, he had genuinely *created* something.

How would that discovery be welcomed? It was a strange new fact: a disconcerting, anarchic fact. Undoubtedly, it would bring forth strong resistance. Physicists attached to the old methods would smile; philosophers would butcher the ears a little more; orators would swing like purring pendulums; jokers would make quips; breathless poets would exhale once again the eternal hymn of the past, covering the tottering idols with flowers.

"And tomorrow, I'll have to reckon with all those chatterboxes!"

Harrisson was stretched out on a low divan at the back of the terrace. The countryside extended before his eyes, calm and sumptuous; a warm breeze was blowing in odorant gusts; the daylight was fading in languorous contentment. Harrisson felt his fatigue dissipating. The old man's last words came to his lips: "Here's the evening...the miraculous and soft evening..."

The young man's gaze settled with respectful affection on the noble pale face with the closed eyes, and he murmured: "The most beautiful brain there ever was! There are dreams in it, miracles...but how weak he is! A hundred years old, alas!"

He recalled the astonishing history of the great Averine, who had already, in the eyes of the masses, taken his place among the figures of legend. Born at the beginning of the fifth century of the Universal Era, abandoned by his parents, completely illiterate at the age of twelve, a kitchen-boy at fifteen, then a cleaner, and then a mechanic, going around the world three or four hundred times aboard the great aerial expresses, he had found himself, at twenty-five, a laboratory assistant in a

Peruvian research institute. People had begun to talk about him in 452; he attracted the attention of the scientific and industrial world by virtue of his discovery of a method of synthesizing albumins a thousand times simpler and more rapid than those previously known. Other discoveries had followed, always presenting the same character of surprising simplicity. Then, in 457, a thunderbolt: the problem of the ether was resolved!

For centuries, the human elite had felt becalmed there, lost in dense mist, at the limits of science and metaphysics. And now a young scientist—well-known, to be sure, but not one of the most famous—had boldly projected an elegant bridge of light toward the inaccessible shore! The ether became a tangible reality, within the jurisdiction of the ordinary procedures of scientific investigation.

All thinking humankind had been shocked by surprise. And then, immediately, passionate and fecund discussions had arisen; theories were confronted, and had crumbled one after another, with a hitherto-unknown rapidity. Since that epoch, a disorderly seething of curiosity had been seen; any audacity had seemed legitimate; the human mind had launched forth into a new and marvelous phase.

Although the work of scientists was disinterested and pure speculation was in honor more than ever, considerable changes nevertheless took place in the march of civilization. Fantastic possibilities appeared on the horizon. There was some anxiety, and even a certain amount of psychological disturbance, but humankind, as a whole, advanced at a brisk pace, with increasing speed, toward an adventurous tomorrow of which no past history could give any idea.

For some time to come, the principal artisan of that formidable evolution would doubtless be that motionless old man, burdened by years, to whom all the scientists on the planet were preparing to pay tribute one more time, on the occasion of his hundredth birthday. The fifth century of the Universal Era would be known as Averine's century. It already was.

Harrisson, the master's favorite pupil and his veritable spiritual heir, was ambitious to continue the great work. He was the director of the Averine Institute, in the former nation of France, celebrated for the richness of its memories, the delicate light of its skies, and the softness of its restful horizons: that charming old nation whose clear language had ended up, after many vicissitudes, imposing itself on the human elite, while English, the first universal language, had rapidly lost its purity and given birth to unstable patois.

Averine lived on the side of a hill, in a rustic house of a frankly archaic style, with a wooden frame, stone walls and a roof of red tiles: a villa to the taste of a modest bourgeois of the decline of the Christian Era. The buildings were surrounded by beautiful grounds. To the right and left, strictly aligned, were other buildings separated by grassy meadows and odorous orchards. For the most part, they were the houses of agriculturalists, very modern and very plush; their metallic roofs gleamed like as many multicolored mirrors. A few artisans or functionaries employed in the industrial power-stations also lived in the area; their more modest houses were aligned perpendicular to the slope or grouped in a fan around the airport that served the locality.

In the depths of the valley a river sparkled. For hundreds of years humans had utilized the eager force of its waters, but modern science had liberated nature. All the hydroelectric installations had disappeared; at least, nothing more remained of them but sparse vestiges, saved by the piety of archeologists: sections of wall invaded by ivy; turbines and dynamos corroded by oxidization; a complicated machinery, puerile and charming, about which poets short of inspiration sang untiringly. The river ran freely between the flowering poplars and enhanced willows whose enormous catkins furnished an inimitable perfume, much sought-after by the elegant.

Before that calm and beautiful landscape, Harrisson daydreamed. An increasing noise caused him to raise his eyes. Among the rapid and silent aircraft, two antique aerobuses, whose silhouettes were vaguely reminiscent of those of birds, were flying low beneath a ceiling of clouds. The *tac-tac* of the electric propeller of the first was audible; the second, even more ancient, which one might have believed to have been taken from a historic museum, progressed thanks to an explosive engine, whose roar filled the air. Luminous banners floated behind the two aerobuses.

Suddenly, as they were passing over the valley, they released fireworks that burst with a soft sound, and a rain of multicolored fire descended.

Averine had raised his head in his turn.

"What's that?" he demanded.

Harrisson went over to him. "I think they're students playing pranks, Master…careless scatterbrains who have unearthed—I don't know where—those hazardous rattletraps in order to startle peaceful people. I've done worse in my time!"

The old man smiled indulgently.

While speaking, Harrisson had flicked a switch and turned the funnel of a receiver toward him. The noise of the motors was muffled, and then suddenly stopped; the two aerobuses were drifting in the wind. Then juvenile voices were heard: songs, and also—which displeased Harrisson—bursts of staccato laughter, abnormal and inextinguishable. It proved, alas, that the new vice, the abuse of exhilarants, had already attained that beautiful youth.

"The fools...the poor fools!" he murmured.

A further rain of sparks was scattered in mid-air, not far from the airport.

Again, Harrison said: "The reckless fools! Just as long as they don't cut off the aerial energy-field with their antediluvian motors and all their scrap metal!"

As he said it, a signal rose up from the neighboring airport; a watchman had spotted the excursionists, and was forbidding access to the danger-zone.

The aerobuses continued to advance, however—and the stop signal appeared again, repeated three times. The watchman was getting annoyed and issuing a threat. Then, there was a storm of jeers from the two aerobuses; whistle-blasts could heard, and animal cries, and then a mocking verse sung in chorus. To the tune of a popular song, in the Old French of the decadence, the students proclaimed the conjugal misfortunes of the airport manager to the face of the heavens.

The aerobuses, rising up ponderously, headed for the clouds.

Darkness had fallen completely. In the heights of the sky, the beacons of isolated aircraft lit up like stars. A long aerial express, bringing yellow workers home, flew eastwards, all its portholes illuminated. On the ground, finally, fluorescent ramps were already festooning a few houses and, at the tops of the tall trees and in the agriculturalists' grounds, photophoric networks disposed like feathers spread a soft blue-tinted light.

Averine got up for dinner.

In the rustic dining-room, the children occupied the places of honor around the master. Samuel was there, and his habitual playmate, Flore, a black girl with enamel-like eyes. There were also local children, round-headed Gauls, noisy and easily amazed. The staff of the house—except for the kitchen staff, who would eat a little later—came immediately after the children. Averine liked young people and working people, simple and ingenuous conversation. For a long time, he had taken pleasure in serving them himself; now he contented himself with gathering them around him, and smiling at their joy.

Harrison occupied the other end of the table, with his companions in labor: two scientists of mature years and a young woman who was scarcely twenty-five, Lygie Rod, already famous for her work on the role of turbulent attractions in the evolution of tumultuous protoplasm. The previous year, Lygie Rod had lost two fingers in a laboratory accident; in her pale, symmetrical face her calm eyes resembled profound wells.

There were only two new guests: a couple passing through who were distantly related to one of the scientists. The man, something of a socialite, was getting bored next to Lygie. The woman, dressed in an antique style, wore her hair long; her dress, generously fissured, allowed the sight of beautifully curved shoulders, painted periwinkle-blue in accordance with the atrocious fashion launched at the beginning of the week by a celebrated Japanese courtesan. Suspended from her left wrist by platinum wire she had a little box containing exhilarating pills. From the start of the meal she had been dipping furtively into the box and, excited by the slight dose of poison, was already laughing at everything, her eyes shining and cheeks red, lovely and disquieting.

An archaic simplicity reigned at Averine's table, and the two strangers, used to the luxury of modern caravanserai, could not believe their eyes. Nevertheless, the fare was abundant and healthy. Save for the enhanced vegetables with transient aromas, which were cooked under pressure at low temperature, the old traditions of French cuisine were maintained in Averine's house.

Fruits covered the table; fruits were a luxury permissible for the humblest. In every country, they arrived from the four corners of the world. In Averine's house, preference was given to the indigenous fruits of the season, furnished by the rich orchards of the neighborhood: enormous brightly-colored fruits with perfumes so varied and so sweet that the ingenuity of chemists had not yet succeeded in imitating them perfectly. There were not only the fruits appreciated by the ancients, but new species obtained by processes of ultra-rapid selection, which produced marvelous results in only a few generations.

Almost all wild fruits, including the most insipid and bitter berries, had attracted the attention of horticulturalists. Even poisonous berries had become large and tasty fruits, keenly sought by gourmets. The hawthorn berry, that of the nightshade, the fruit of the sweet-briar, the pine-cone and the horse-chestnut figured on the best tables as well as the poorest.

For a week, Harrisson, whose work had occupied him to the point of making him forget meals, had been living on beech-nuts in the depths of his laboratory. This evening, by contrast, the scientist, filled with joy by his victory, appreciated the food as a connoisseur; he relaxed, displaying the joviality of insouciance.

Lygie's eyes met his; he divined their mute interrogation. Leaning toward the young woman, he murmured: "Yes! I think success is within our grasp."

In a low voice, Lygie replied: "Congratulations! It's a great accomplishment!"

"It's as much your accomplishment as mine, Lygie!"

A flicker of joy lit up in the calm eyes, but it was brief. The young woman lowered her pale forehead, and only a slight tremor in her hands still revealed hr emotion.

In the same confidential tone, Harrisson went on: "For the moment, please be discreet...especially in front of that crackbrain..."

The female stranger was laughing, her head tipped back, her gaze intoxicated. Anticipating a further gesture toward the box of poison, Harrisson offered her the first slice of an enormous and appetizing Breton acorn that had just been served—and he recited, in a joyful voice, the lines of a gourmand poet who had celebrated that modern fruit, the bread of the poor and the banquet of the rich, the preferred aliment of the very young and very old alike. All the guests applauded and raised their glasses to Harrisson. Myrtle wine, sparkling and perfumed, quivered in rustic goblets of rose crystal.

At a stroke from the kitchen bell, the meal concluded. The two laboratory assistants and Lygie immediately rose to their feet in order to go in their turn to serve the kitchen workers.

Having taken their leave of Averine, the two guests withdrew. The young woman wanted to visit an exhibition of hats and then go to an aerial rally above the Archipelago. The man grumbled, saying that he had just gone almost all the way around the world, which seemed to him to be enough for one day, and that he felt no need to spend half the night in the clouds. He would have preferred to go directly back to the Azores, where they lived. He ended up giving in.

Harrisson accompanied the guests to their aircraft. It was a luxury two-seater, elongated in the form of a cigar and quilted with compressed oxygen. The disintegration of a potassium salt provided heat, lighting and motive force; slowed down or accelerated at will, it permitted nonchalant strolling as well as meteoric speed. Thanks to an exceedingly simple mechanism, one could also utilize the energy of the public lines.

Having raided her little box once again, the young woman extended her hand to Harrisson, then stretched out on her cushions. The man, lying down in the prow, was already maneuvering the delicate levers. The hood came down and the apparatus rose up vertically, between the trees in the grounds; after a few seconds of slow oblique progress, its speed increased rapidly. The aircraft flew eastwards, passing like a meteor over the zone of the large expresses.

Harrison went back to the villa and went into the library. After a few moments, the two laboratory assistants joined him there. Harrison's success was also theirs, to some extent; excitement and fatigue made their faces pale. Wearied by the work of the preceding days, they soon retired to bed.

Left alone, Harrisson opened a window. It was still warm; a mild night enveloped the world. Devoid of photophoric networks, the trees in the grounds interlaced their dark branches. At dusk, the birds of the neighborhood came to take refuge there, while disquieting lights came on in the orchards, the greenhouses and the agriculturalists' fields. Facing the window, in an old wild oak, a nightingale began to sing. The villa was at rest; all the receivers were switched off; distant noises no longer reached it. Alone in the midst of the silence, that little song spread out like an ardent flower from a calyx of shadow.

The foliage of the rustic garden masked the horizon, and only a diffuse light rose up from the surrounding countryside. High in the sky, rare and silent aircraft were passing over, their lights scintillating like stars. The serenity of the moment was such that one might have believed that one had gone back in time. Ten centuries before, in the twentieth of the Christian Era, there might have been a house like Averine's at that point on the earth's surface, and large wild trees in which, on beautiful summer evenings, nightingales came to sing...

In spite of human industry, in spite of the immense efforts of human beings, certain aspects of the world remained the same; certain scenes were renewed, little different from one era to the next.

Harrisson smiled, and thought: *There's a theme as banal as one could wish, which I might suggest to our Lahorie...but he's already used it a hundred times!*

He closed the window and started thinking about the life of the people who had inhabited the region a thousand years before...

His thoughts did not linger long in that vague reverie. The sudden flickering of a malfunctioning photophore brought his attention back to a precise question. He wondered whether, in the twentieth century of the preceding era, the ancient phosphorescent lamp—the first attempt at rational lighting—had been in current use. Several scientific works, rapidly consulted, did not clarify the matter. He searched the bottom shelves of the library, to which were relegated the principal contemporary works and a few works of philosophy and history.

His eyes lighted upon *A General History of Civilization, from the eighteenth century A.D. to the fifth century U.E.* It was a considerable work, printed in violet on unoxidizable metal, counting no less than two thousand pages of densely-packed text. In spite of the extreme thinness of the pages and the lightness of the porous aluminum binding, it weighed about as much as an ancient pocket-book printed on thick paper.

Harrisson opened the book. The historian was no more explicit than the scientists. He mentioned "electric lighting" several times, but that vague term, which could be applied to mercury lamps, might as easily describe various more primitive methods of lighting—such as, for instance, simple incandescent lamps with metallic filaments.

Nevertheless, Harrisson continued leafing through the book, the tone of which pleased him. Writing the history of humankind in the scientific age, the author, with implacable logic, demonstrated that, at the origin of every change in the progress of civilization, a discovery was found of which, very often, no one had at first perceived the importance. Contrary to several of his colleagues, the historian maintained that neither philosophers nor moralists, poets, warriors and legislators guided humankind, their personal actions being only secondary, temporary local and short-term. The true directors were the modest seekers of whom their contemporaries were scarcely aware, and who were pursuing their disinterested research in the silence of laboratories. Each of their deeds echoed to infinity; the most seemingly-insignificant discovery had the potential to shake the entire social edifice.

The Author classified events in a new schema, according to their true import. Thus, in the nineteenth century of the Christian Era, he placed little emphasis on the emancipation of the masses and the sentimental rivalries of peoples; the major occurrence was the scientific awakening of the more powerful nations, the utilization—still very primitive—of steam and electricity. An important date in human history was also to be found in the nineteenth century; in the year 1867 the French scientist Niepce de Saint-Victor had discovered, by chance, the radioactivity of uranium salts, and that discovery, which passed completely unnoticed at the time, now appeared at least as important as the discovery of fire by the primal horde.[5]

The beginning of the twentieth century also marked an important date. A millenarian dream was finally realized: aerial navigation commenced—a dangerous and costly navigation, it is true, only utilizing primitive means, and which, in spite of rapid progress, only played a secondary role in the European war of 1914-1918.

The historian briefly mentioned that long and bloody skirmish, whose causes seemed, at a distance, puerile and extremely confused. Nothing new, in any

---

[5] The photographic pioneer Abel Niepce de Saint-Victor did indeed observe, in 1857 rather than the 1867 quoted by Pérochon, that photographic emulsions could be exposed even in complete darkness in proximity to certain salts, and eventually fixed the blame on uranium salts, to which he attributed a hitherto-unknown form of radiation. His employer, Michel Chevreuil, hailed the discovery as fundamental and Niepce was in no doubt about its importance, but no one else took the slightest notice, and it was not until the sensation following the discovery of X-rays in 1895 that Henri Bequerel "discovered" the radioactivity of uranium for a second time, in 1896.

case, had emerged during the war—only a few timid excursions of aircraft in the background, and a few ferocious but maladroit deployments of poison gases. As in the remotest times, the belligerents had sent their most vigorous young males against the enemy, confiding firearms to them, resulting in a terrible negative selection. That war, pursued for long months with a terrible obstinacy by numerous armies, marvelously disciplined and provided with murderous engines, had severely shaken the old world.

The magnitude of the catastrophe should have caused the scales to fall from the blindest eyes, but it had not. People had not understood that a new era was beginning, in which prudence, for want of generosity, would become an essential virtue. As soon as the armed conflict was over, the conflicts of pride or self-interest had enfevered hearts again; again, hands that were still bloody had clenched into threatening fists. Never, perhaps, had humans been so lacking in clear-sightedness and good will than at that point in time.

Science was progressing rapidly, but few people thought of being surprised or mistrustful. Intelligence seemed somewhat dazed or disorientated. Military leaders were seen gravel drafting treatises on strategy imitative of antiquity for the use of the warriors of the future. Philosophers ratiocinated; poets stammered; squadrons of myopics occupied the sentry-boxes and blockaded the crossroads of thought. In more than one country, vulgar demagogues hoisted themselves on to popular stages; semi-madmen brandishing clubs succeeded in finding an audience. The masses, still numbed by shock, and sensing confusedly that the world was changing, were hesitant. Uniquely concerned with the immediate future, they lost their ancient virtues without acquiring new ones, and let things happen with a sort of disenchanted fatalism. No nation knew exactly where it wanted to go.

The end of the twentieth century and the first half of the twenty-first were an epoch of disorderly social experiments. One after another, powerful collectives fell apart. Civil wars succeed national wars. A summary conception of justice rendered them frequent and fierce. They broke out for absurd or futile reasons. With the intention of avoiding some insignificant malaise, people did not hesitate to unleash the worst catastrophes.

Properly speaking, there were no longer any armies or fronts in warfare. The entire population was afflicted, the entire country ravaged. Delicate and powerful engines, which could easily be handled by women or children, dealt death at long distances. Firearms were still utilized, but gradually lost their importance. Toxic gases were killing many people; aircraft carrying explosives or various poisons flattened cities or rendered them uninhabitable. Several times over, microbial disseminations depopulated vast regions, and the scourge threatened the entire world.

In spite of all those upheavals, humankind seemed to be making progress. Science, which armed people so terribly for evil purposes, also armed them for virtuous ones. The masses were less harshly subjected to the law of toil. The satisfaction of primordial needs became increasingly easy. The most humble rarely knew great deprivation; in periods of peace, even though rusticity diminished and new artificial needs were generated, a certain economic ease was within the range of everyone. Humankind evolved in fits and starts toward a future of practical median contentment—and individual morality, in the more powerful nations, seemed to improve gradually.

In the twenty-second century, in the old countries of Europe and America, where in spite of the mixture of races, white men were still dominant, a new order was finally established. No one there dared to adopt an aggressive chauvinism or spitefully extol class struggle. For want of warm sympathy between different groups of human beings, the instinct of self-preservation muffled impacts, promoted tolerance and reciprocal concessions. Although equality did not exist anywhere in actuality, at least appearances were very nearly saved, between individuals and between States. The population of the white race formed a vast federation of egalitarian republics, with common interests and conciliatory tendencies.

Facing them was the bloc of yellow peoples. Science, like the flourish of a magic wand, had extracted them from a long torpor. The awakening had been prodigious. Their scientists were equal in reputation to the scientists of Europe and America; their industrialists, businessmen and bankers invaded all the markets of the globe; at the same time, an unprecedented artistic renaissance coincided among them with a moral depravity that astonished the old world. Arrived too rapidly at scientific civilization, also afflicted with powerful xenophobic associations, those audacious and turbulent peoples brought the perpetual threat of grave disorder.

At the beginning of the twenty-second century war broke out. A Manchu physicist had discovered a rapid method of manufacturing gold, and the Asiatic bankers profited from the temporary disturbance of commercial relations to reduce certain collectives in Africa and Asia to virtual slavery. At the Council of Nations, the prudence of diplomats pacified the conflict, but the whites were obliged to concede great advantages to their adversaries.

Fifteen years later there was a further alert, again occasioned by an important scientific development capable of immediate application. It was a matter of the discovery in certain strata of the Orinoco basin of a metal akin to lead—it was initially named Lead Z—which had the property of disintegrating at an easily-regulated rate under the influence of appropriate radiations. There was a possibility of obtaining in the near future, among other things, explosives of perfect stability and formidable power.

The Asiatic financiers, immediately alerted—and more ambitious and arrogant than ever—employed intermediaries to buy the totality of the mineral deposits. The danger seemed so great, however, that the entire world was troubled. Once again, the Council of Nations found a compromise: the mines would be nationalized. In reality, the Asiatics kept the lion's share; supervising the production and dominating the market, they even set out to establish clandestine stocks before other deposits were discovered, or further scientific discoveries averted the threat. These advantages did not seem sufficient to them. A minority of nationalist megalomaniacs provoked violent troubles in southern China. The regional diplomats who had signed the accord sat in judgment, and a number of people were executed.

A female Laotian poet, as famous for her pride and debauchery as for her extravagant lyricism, set herself at the head of the discontented. At her instigation, a semi-secret society was formed—the Cut-Cut—which soon brought together a hundred million fanatics. Propagated by writers and orators of barbaric eloquence, the worst insanities of ancient chauvinist and bellicose literature became articles of faith for its initiates. So, although the great majority of people remained peaceful, abominable adventures seemed inevitable.

The war broke out in 2145, with no other immediate cause than an immodest act by a woman.

One evening in May, the female poet Lia-Te, having had a whim to appear in the nude, riding a goat, at a sermon given by a clergyman in San Francisco, was escorted back to her aircraft amid a storm of jeers.

Scarcely was she aboard than she raced to the telephone, and, in grandiloquent phrases uttered in a furious voice, informed the Cut-Cut of the insult suffered by its president. Immediately alerted, five hundred aircraft took off and crossed the Pacific. A few hours later, San Francisco woke up beneath a deluge of asphyxiating and incendiary bombs. Only ten thousand inhabitants survived the attack.

There was a moment of stupor throughout the world.

At the Council of Nations, the Asiatic diplomats, receiving contradictory instructions from their respective countries, hesitated. When a decision was finally taken to punish the guilty and dissolve their organization, precious time had been lost; the Cut-Cut were masters of the situation. The whites in Asia were already being hunted down; many of them, delivered to the fury of the populace, found death in tortures of unprecedented cruelty. The old leavens of martial madness boiled over, rising up in bloody foam. Menacing clamors flew from continent to continent; all the telephones on the planet resounded with Homeric insults.

Finally, attacked by an airborne squadron from Indo-China, the whites of Australia riposted energetically. The real war began.

The historian distinguished three acts in that great drama of the twilight of the Christian Era.

In the beginning, the Asiatics, provided with powerful factories and superbly-equipped laboratories, had the clear advantage, but not without suffering serious damage themselves. That initial period was marked by the destruction of great cities. No defenses could provide efficacious protection for New York, Buenos Aires, London, Paris, Melbourne and Cape Town against the aerial squadrons of the yellow peoples. In the other camp, Peking, Canton, Hai-Phong and Calcutta fared no better.

After a year of conflict, a large number of Chinese, Japanese and Indian factories were still intact, while the strength of the whites was diminishing rapidly. The Asiatic aircraft had begun the methodical destruction of secondary nuclei of resistance. The whites and their allies, the blacks, seemed doomed to total defeat and enslavement.

Then the face of things changed abruptly.

A young French physicist, Noelle Roger,[6] had just perfected, in the greatest secrecy, an elegant and simple means of defense. Directing over long distances a beam

---

[6] The choice of this name might not have been accidental; "Noelle Roger" was the pseudonym of Hélène Pittard (1874-1953), a notable Swiss writer of *romans scientifiques* who had published an apocalyptic novel of her own, *Le Nouveau déluge* [The New Deluge], in 1922 and a significant novel of superhumanity, *Le Nouvel Adam* (tr. as *The New Adam*) in 1924. The generally alarmist tone of her works is not dissimilar to that of the present novel. Her later works included *Le Soleil enseveli* [The Shrouded Sun] (1928) and *Le Chercheur d'ondes* [The Wave-Seeker] (1931).

of parallel waves hitherto unknown to nature, it provoked the deflagration of any and all explosives.

Immediately after the first trials, a battery of emissive apparatus and projectors was constituted and entrusted to a crew of specialist electricians commanded by Noelle Roger in person. The effect of the surprise attack was formidable and unprecedented.

The historian placidly reported that first appearance of Roger projectors as it was mentioned in contemporary chronicles.

Coming from Asia Minor, an immense squadron of sweeper aircraft was flying over the archipelago at the fortieth parallel, advancing toward Mount Olympus, the point of separation. It was intended to administer the *coup-de-grâce* to the whites of southern Europe. The Asiatics were flying in broad daylight, in tight formation, sure of their force, taking no precautions. Behind a small hill in Thessaly, not far from the coast, ten electricians were waiting, lying in the bottom of a trench beside their batteries of projectors. Standing in the middle of them, Noelle Roger scrutinized the sky.

Suddenly, she raised her hand. The electricians to her left and right unmasked their projectors. Instantaneously, a mighty explosion rent the air; all the aircraft on the right flank had blown up at the same time. The aircraft in the center, blown sideways by the blast, fluttered like dead leaves; surrounded by a sudden fog, they switched on their searchlights and launched rockets, seeking the invisible enemy at random.

Then the young Frenchwoman, emerging from the trench, advanced toward the top of the hill. Half-turning to her companions, her eyes excited and her mouth grim, she pointed to the horizon with an ardent sweeping gesture, and shouted at the top of her voice:

"From north to south, mow them down!"

A thousand aircraft, each carrying a ton of explosives of terrible power, were annihilated simultaneously. The earth trembled. A whirlwind descended upon the land and threw the sea to assault the shore. The electricians, plastered to the floor of the trench, saw Noelle Roger lifted from the ground, her arms still raised. They found her a hundred meters away, lying dead, face upwards, her mouth still howling, with an indescribable horror in the depths of her inhuman eyes.

Of the immense air-fleet nothing remained but a vast and vague cloud on the horizon.

From that moment on the fate of the war seemed to be settled.

The Antipodeans were not discouraged, however. Their constructors were working feverishly; for every aircraft destroyed ten emerged from the factories. At the same time, the offensive tactics changed; they no longer attacked except in darkness, in widely dispersed order, seeking surprise everywhere. All their scientists devoted themselves to the problem of the Roger waves. In vain, on their advice, attempts were made to bury stocks of explosives, to sink them under water, to protect them by continuous metal envelopes; the new radiations seemed to be endowed with universal penetration. Then the Asiatic physicists studied and perfected methods permitting the utilization of lead Z, on which the Roger waves had no effect. The near-instantaneous disintegration of the metal permitted the shortage of explosives to be compensated, but the meager stocks were soon exhausted.

The whites took the offensive in their turn. Their offers of peace having been disdainfully rejected, they assembled their last remaining aircraft and submarines and mounted destructive raids. Reflectors of great power swept considerable area, destroying ammunition depots, shattering loaded weapons and annihilating police forces, whose cartridges exploded. Ahead of the invaders they created a zone deprived of explosives, in which only toxic gases were still to be feared; soon, the centers of production had been located, and that danger too was nullified.

One after another, the Asiatic factories were blown up, set ablaze or pulverized.

Again, the whites offered peace; their enemies replied by torturing to death the prisoners they still had hidden in the depths of mines. That was the signal for violent reprisals.

The last Asian cities went up in flames; one night, Anglo-Saxon engineers smashed the dams of an immense reservoir on the inferior stream of the Hoang-Ho, and the river, immediately changing its course, devastated the most heavily-populated region in the world.

The second phase of the war was completed by that terrible drowning.

At that point, perhaps a hundred million people had already perished. Reserves of every sort were exhausted; the specter of famine loomed large—and yet, the bellicose fury did not die down. The Asiatics, especially, were prey to an insensate rage. Their scientists were still searching for the secret of the Roger waves or, at least, some efficacious response; their demagogue exalted the pride of the race; moribund poets gave voice to demented songs.

When all hope of victory was lost, the yellow races unleashed microbial warfare. Siberian aircraft with their armaments removed, disguised as ambulances, sowed Europe, Africa, America and Australia with carefully-selected pathogenic species of unprecedented virulence.

And that was the third phase of the war, much the most terrible.

Until then, every time a microbial attack had been launched, humankind had easily localized the scourge, but this time, all the races were at the end of their tether, breathless and bloodless. The general destruction of cities, the annihilation of hospitals and principal laboratories had been sufficient to render any methodical plan of defense inapplicable. In addition, rapid means of communication were lacking. Railways, in effect, no longer existed; roads, cut at many points, were only of use to old short-range automobiles; steamships lay at the bottom of the sea; even aircraft were scarce. Finally, the radiotelephonic stations, targeted at the outset of hostilities and soon destroyed, had only been replaced by ramshackle installations of limited power.

Humankind, out of breath, was like a huge exhausted body, its reactions confused and awkward.

The scourge rapidly infected the entire world. Soon, no further conflict was possible. New diseases made their appearance; other, reputedly benign, assumed destructive forms. Some regions lost almost all their inhabitants. Everywhere, decomposing corpses strewed the countryside.

The war was over; death alone had triumphed. Ten years after the outbreak of the first epidemic, the Earth had lost more than a third of its population; six hundred millions human beings had died. The survivors were battling against famine and reverting to primitive forms of life. Here and there, tribes were living by hunting and fishing; others were beginning to drive flocks from pasture to pasture. Marauders gathered around petty chiefs sowed terror. The strongest, the wiliest and the cruelest were already beginning to form a proud and cynical aristocracy of sorts.

Civilization seemed to have disappeared for centuries. The Christian Era concluded with a confused twilight overhung by an immense odor of cadavers.

And yet, three hundred years later, a new dawn appeared...

The historian emphasized the cause of that astonishing renaissance.

In spite of appearances, the final epoch of barbarity different from the earlier epochs. It was a kind of coma succeeding a grave illness, a formidable crisis provoked by the revolutionary appearance of science. Science was not dead, however; the flame had flickered without going out. Soon, all the lights began to reignite. The scientists had only to search the past and reconnect the broken threads.

Finally instructed by recent and frightful experience, however, humankind was about to take a new path and make a great effort of adaptation.

Humans remained egotistical and cruel; even though a great deal was expected of science, no one could yet nurture the hope of rapidly modifying the nature of the individual. In order to render martial adventures less probable, a clear-sighted elite admitted the necessity of artificially forming broad currents of opinion, creating a new moral atmosphere—even if it were necessary, in order to do that, to sacrifice some precious living strength.

At any rate, obedient to a profound instinct of self-preservation, humankind rejected concepts that had once been tutelary but had become dangerous to the species in an epoch of scientific civilization.

The idea of nationality was no longer found in the heart of the masses, having become somnolent; pride of caste was a capital sin. Historical studies, creative of troubled states of mind among the humble, were only permitted to a small number of mature individuals, who had to undertake never to seek any public office.

A new classification of virtues and vices came into effect. The necessity of generosity took on the evidence of a mathematical verity. Urgent apostles preached prudence, tolerance and moderation, and innumerable radiophones repeated their sermons.

The doctrine of courage raised a few debates, but the majority of moralists agreed in recognizing, in that great virtue of the Christian Era, a mild form of ancestral ferocity. In the same way that ferocity had seemed dangerous since the dawn of historic ages, certain forms of courage seemed obsolete, redoubtable and bound to disappear in the scientific epoch. On that point, evolution was not only to continue but to accelerate rapidly.

They circled around the instinct of justice delicately. That was a matter of a recent acquisition of the human mind. Prehistoric humans would probably have derided the idea of law, or been unable to conceive of it. By contrast, in spite of appearances, the people of the Christian Era headed directly toward what they called justice. They went by hazardous routes, in which abrupt detours were by no means rare, but they went passionately, and it was almost always in the name of justice that they killed.

That instinct, in its full growth, returned forcefully after the catastrophe; the young god conserved his worshipers. Meanwhile, ideal justice, a white summit raising its vague silhouette in the mist, still seemed inaccessible, as far away as ever from vulgar reality. Of that discord between human aspirations and facts, danger might be born. Great efforts were made to organize a society in which all the appearances of law were preserved, and which nominally satisfied the universal need for equality, a summary form of the desire for justice among the masses. There could no longer be any question of superior peoples, privileged races or governing classes. Only the supremacy of wisdom was recognized and tolerated, by means of numerous real and illusory guarantees.

Humankind gave itself willingly to experienced leaders of proven prudence, whose primary role was conciliation. In anticipation of disorders, these chiefs also had that their disposal powerful mean of coercion. After several premature and fruitless attempts, three hundred years after the destruction of San Francisco, the Supreme Council of the planet met and held its first session on the very location of the obliterated city.

The Universal Era began.

Harrisson closed the book. He knew the rest: the history of the humankind of the Universal Era was, in effect, nothing other than the history of science. The only important dates of that era were marked by resounding discoveries.

In the first two centuries, the efforts of researchers had been primarily devoted to artificial disintegration. The second century had seen important realizations: the substitution of formidable intra-atomic energies for ordinary sources of heat, light and electricity, and the production of new radiations facilitating the transmutation, perfection and vulgarization of the cinetelephone.[7]

---

[7] The word "television" did exist in 1925; indeed, Pérochon actually uses it a few paragraphs further on, but only once,

The third and fourth centuries had been marked by the considerable progress of biology, medicine and experimental psychology.

The fifth had been illuminated by Averine's endeavors. The sixth was finally opening on vast horizons. The old theory of the degradation of energy was giving way to infinitely audacious concepts; the possibility of creation had appeared. Curtains that had previously been utterly opaque were being ripped apart; humankind appeared to be approaching the metaphysical era.

During those five centuries, the march of civilization had been narrowly determined by the progress of the sciences. Social organization, in the year 525, bore little resemblance to that of the later Christian ages. In that distant epoch it had seemed that cities would gradually absorb the whole population of the planet. The cities sacked during the final torment had not been rebuilt on their ruins, however; the words "city-dweller" and "country-dweller" no longer had any meaning in the Universal Era.

Atomic disintegration having put a prodigious quantity of energy at the fortunate disposal of humankind, engineers had surrounded the Earth with a network of zones of force almost corresponding to the ancient

---

probably not intending the meaning we now attach to the word. The possibility of broadcasting pictures was more often envisaged in the early 1920s as a potential improvement of the already familiar telephone rather than an augmentation of not-yet-familiar broadcast radio, hence Pérochon's slightly eccentric neologism for a hypothetical system that combines the functions of our televisions and telephones. That might seem more appropriate and far-sighted now that mobile phones have televisual capabilities, although the miniaturization of the technology is one thing that he did not anticipate.

system of meridians and parallels; between the principal lines, secondary lines were found at one-minute intervals. That immense public network furnished the necessary energy gratuitously to the aerial, terrestrial and maritime transportation serves, to the radiophone and television services, and, in general, to all the ordinary means of existence. Agricultural and industrial enterprises, which required considerable energy, also profited from the proximity of the zones. All the motors currently in usage were regulated by the public motors, producing or utilizing the same forms of energy and only differing in power.

Thus, humankind had been invincibly led to build according to a linear plan, with no great city comparable the monstrous cities of the anterior epoch, but only a few smaller agglomerations, routinely build in a fan around airports. There were interminable files of habitations everywhere in proximity to the major lines, generally more widely-spaced along the secondary lines. Within the general repertoire of the planet, every house and establishment had a number that immediately indicated its exact position. Thus, the Averine Institute—the laboratory and the house—bore the number 1.47.12.32.007. Known throughout the entire world, it was commonly known as 1.47.[8]

For five centuries, no serious disturbance had posed a serious threat to civilization. The vigilance of the Supreme Council generally prevented conflicts. When wars

---

[8] The region where the author was born and lived is just to the south of the 47th parallel, but much closer to the Greenwich meridian than one degree of east longitude. It is conceivable, however, that the novel's zero meridian is the Paris meridian rather than the Greenwich meridian.

broke out in spite of everything—that had happened several times in the early centuries—they were stifled immediately, no matter what the cost, by the universal police.

The human elite, in its entirety, had become resolutely hostile to any kind of martial adventure. The Earth was repopulated fairly rapidly. Wise people led the new generations prudently toward a tranquil and reasonable future.

And yet, people were unacquainted with happiness!

The curse of the era was a profound sadness that took the form, among the elite, of an incurable pessimism, and which struck the masses, perhaps even more cruelly, with a kind of senility of the heart. True joy—warm, creative joy—was scarcely encountered, except in certain scientists. Literature and the arts were in complete decadence. The semi-barbaric epoch of the Christian twilight had seen the production of incomparable poems, undoubtedly the most beautiful that had ever soothed human suffering. Those poems were repeated and imitated without understanding then—or, rather, in the guise of refinement and delicacy, poets descended into obscure complication.

The outmoded virtues—the virile religion of effort, the peevish religion of honor, the brutal love of justice, the contrary and no less brutal desire for domination, an irrational appetite for risk and adventure; all the dangerous virtues rejected by the instinct of conservation—were cruelly lacking in the new humankind. Souls deprived of anxiety languished, like plants transplanted from the open air into the tranquil atmosphere of a greenhouse. Exactly like the artists, the populace, whose life was easy, slipped into a profound *ennui*, into morbid passions and sentimental monstrosities.

The harmful use of exhilarating pills had spread in spite of all imaginable regulations. Semi-secret associations devoted themselves to the most wretched debaucheries. A frightful sadism appeared in some individuals. Elsewhere, by virtue of a singular regression, explosions of collective brutality often occurred among the masses. The most popular spectacles were those of the arena; for those games, carnivorous species that would otherwise have disappeared long ago were carefully conserved, at great expense, in the parks of Africa and Asia. Some gladiators rapidly became the idols of the public. When they confronted the wild beasts, a simple wooden club in their hand, radiophones carried the frantic acclamations and howling of delirious crowds to the four corners of the earth.

For more than half a century, however, a new and rapid evolution of mores had been manifest. Averine's discoveries had had unexpected repercussions. They had given the mind an abrupt jolt; with a sharp shock, they had broken the panes of the greenhouse. Thanks to them, the world would perhaps know once again the torment of hazardous horizons; once again, alas, clouds might accumulate, heavy with unforeseen storms.

The danger was obvious to the thoughtful Harrisson.

Humankind, artificially moderated and artificially aged, had gradually recovered its imprudent youth during the last fifty years. Recent philosophers had denied the pessimism that had darkened the previous ages; poets were reigniting the flames of enthusiasm. A muted process of renewal was operating within the masses. Without renouncing the vices they had recently acquired, the people were listening in their hearts to the hot and troubling voices of repressed instincts. Confused and fundamentally brutal aspirations were aggregating in vague and simple ideas. The words *justice, honor* and *liberty* were beginning once again to flap like flags, in arrogant speeches. All kinds of regionalist concepts were attracting the adhesion of crowds. On the margins of the law, corporations were organizing themselves combatively; partial strikes were breaking out—not, for the most part, for economic reasons, but with regard to paltry questions of precedence.

The inhabitants of the southern hemisphere—less numerous than those of the northern hemisphere, and consequently drawing less from the public reserves of energy—were claiming and demanding honorific compensations. Within the same region, competitions of self-regard or self-interest were giving birth to analogous conflicts between the users of the secondary lines and those of the major lines. Furthermore, in all the countries in the world, a muted rivalry that was growing incessantly was setting the inhabitants of latitudinal zones against those of longitudinal zones—a rivalry so absurd that no one, to begin with, had attached any great importance to it. The word, however, had gradually created the thing.

Without any serious reason, the workers in the power-generating industries, the functionaries of businesses or manual enterprises, building workers, meteorological contractors and those in aerial transport were installing themselves preferentially along lines of latitude. On the other hand, the great agriculturalists, engineers, organizers of transport by land and sea, civil servants, domestic workers and those involved in warehousing and distributing goods were mostly on the meridians. Increasingly clear differences were appearing between the two groups. The appetite for conflict, an unadmitted but profound cause, was creating a schism and heterogeneity, and the formation of opposable camps. In spite of all the efforts of the supreme power, the movement was increasing rapidly.

Finally, the idea of fatherland was reborn, with all its ancient force.

At the apogee of Christian civilization, the increasing rapidity of means of communication had seemed bound to lead eventually to a complete fusion of races. That had not happened; the mixture remained entirely superficial. In the modern epoch, one could even observe an inverse and apparently paradoxical phenomenon. Traveling around the planet with a previously-inconceivable rapidity and in conditions of perfect comfort and security, people returned faithfully to their home ground. Every evening, the great aerial expresses took innumerable workers home from one continent to another. No one any longer experienced the need to move abroad; the extreme facility of communications impeded the slow migrations that had had the only durable effects of the intermingling of races.

Thus, the different human groups were separating again. As in the Christian Era, white people lived in Europe and America, yellow people in Asia. Turbulent republics were forming in Africa. Some peoples had begun to elect particular assemblies as well as their delegates to the World Parliaments. Experiments in national legislation of a disquieting disparity were being superimposed on universal legislation. Ancient local customs were reemerging from forgetfulness. The Minister of Public Festivities, whose role had been very important in previous centuries, was seeing his efforts annihilated by general indifference; only regional festivals were celebrated with gusto.

Legends of obscure origin delighted the masses. Among the whites of Europe, *The Heroism of Noelle Roger*, a long barbaric and naïve poem, was enriched on a daily basis by anonymous supplements. In the same way, among the Asiatics, popular sentiment took to heart the mysteriously-born *Epic of Lia-Te*, the primitive poet of the heroic era.

It was in this fashion that a dull seething of souls was manifest everywhere.

The disconcerting character of recent scientific discoveries rendered a new effort of adaptation indispensable—but it was precisely at the present moment, when prudence was becoming increasingly necessary, that humankind seemed to want to fall back into ancient errors, and to set off recklessly along the old paths of adventure.

To be sure, modern society had proved itself. It was a complicated and robust organism, richly innervated, all of whose parts put themselves on the defensive at the slightest alert. Thus far, wars had been immediately localized and stifled—but would that always be the case in future?

One could hope that humankind, in case of trouble, would avoid the known dangers, would resist primitive forces without too much difficulty—but there was no proof that it would not be exposed one day to the threat of new and prodigiously subtle elements.

That was not a gratuitous hypothesis. Scientists of Averine's school were studying such elements. They were witnessing miraculous syntheses, the birth of theories escaping ordinary laws and anticipating magical periods when energy would increase to a higher degree and in which the progress of phenomena might be disrupted in defiance of all logic.

Starting from what had once been conventionally known as the etheric void, Harrisson had been the first to obtain, at the price of an insignificant initial stimulus, rapidly-rotating regradatory[9] vortices, whose ultimate term was a mixture of unstable gases or an impalpable and spontaneously radioactive metallic dust. For several years, Harrisson had been studying the radiation of these artificial systems and its action on colloids. Ingeniously isolating each radiation and eliminating antagonistic actions, he had observed the appearance of numerous living organisms, almost all of which seemed to react to unknown astronomical influences.

The life thus created offered extremely diverse characteristics. The ordinary life of terrestrial beings only represented one variety, and a mediocre one at that, much less interesting for a scientist than those grouped under the general headings of intermediary life, uniform life and tumultuous life. Tumultuous protoplasm, of which Harrisson had made a particular study, exhibited disconcerting properties, reacting with prodigious vivacity to the influence of ordinary physical agents, bringing about strange transmutations productive of energy, and, finally, provoking profound disturbances in

---

[9] I have anglicized the improvised term *regradateurs*, which evidently derives from *grade* [rank]. The theory of matter tacitly developed here is essentially Cartesian, imagining centers of gravity as disturbances of a fundamental ether, analogous to whirlpools in water, but it modernizes such notions by adding on a more complex theory of radiations associated with different kinds (or "grades") of matter, each associated with a different kind of life.

organisms endowed with ordinary life: rapid agglutination, or the unexpected proliferation of certain cellular elements.

New sciences were about to be born; great and numerous problems were arising—and Harrison wondered whether he might be about to confront some immense danger. Already, in the third and fourth centuries, biology, medicine and psychology had reached dead ends several times over. Might the audacious enterprises of the physicists of the sixth lead humankind to the edge of the precipice?

At the beginning of the new century, science appeared yet again to have a disquieting revolutionary face. Would the necessary adaptation have time to occur?

It seemed pointless to count on an interruption of scientific progress; curiosity would never step back the threshold of the unknown. On the other hand, experience proved that neither was it was necessary to rely too much on the great artificial currents of opinion to precipitate the evolution of popular sentiments. Whatever was attempted, the heart lagged behind the mind; discord was doubtless as old as the world, but it might become fatal if it were accentuated.

For humanity to be able to endure, sheltered from storms, it required an ever-increasing prudence and an ever-present vigilance. Modern society ought, before anything else, to maintain close surveillance of scientific research, but nothing was being done. Under the pretext of individual liberty, scientists remained masters of their actions, just like the most inoffensive of mortals—and there was nothing to prevent the action of an imprudent individual or a madman from unleashing some terrible catastrophe.

Harrison thought about his earliest endeavors; he too had made his discoveries known without envisaging all the possible consequences. Since then, numerous scientists had taken the hazardous path that he had traced prematurely.

Harrisson reflected further, and grave anxiety tarnished the joy of his recent success. He promised himself to be more prudent than before, and congratulated himself on not having said anything at dinner in the presence of the socialite with the periwinkle breasts.

So long as that is produced before my eyes on a small scale, he thought, *the danger isn't very serious!*

Although it was already late, he stood up, with the intention of going down to the laboratory again.

At that moment, a bell rang faintly. Harrison went to the back of the room and pressed a small metal lever; immediately, on the screen of the unmasked cinetelephone, the dancer Sylvia appeared. She was an Egyptian, famed for her beauty, her talent and a few resounding adventures, notably with the poet Lahorie and a famous gladiator, for whom she had fought a duel. For several weeks she had been pursuing Harrisson, and not seeking to hide the fact.

The young scientist bowed gallantly before the apparatus and murmured a banal compliment.

"Do you know," demanded Sylvia, immediately, "whether I shall be asked to dance at Averine's hundredth birthday party?"

"Can you doubt it?" Harrisson replied. "You'll be the queen of the celebrations. You'll dance before the eyes of innumerable crowds—for the entire world. And all the white-haired old scientists..."

"Enough!" she said. "No impertinence. I scorn crowds, and white-haired old scientists even more so…let's talk seriously. It's you who'll have the honors of the day, for the miraculous work that you've mentioned to me vaguely. Yes, yes! Don't shake your head! You'll be triumphant. I want that! I do!" With a rapid gesture, she cast off the scarf that was covering her admirable blue shoulders. "So," she said, "I can count on you not to forget me?"

"Don't worry! Not if they postpone the festival for a hundred years!"

"Thank you. You're an adorable great scientist! I shan't dance for the entire world, but for you—for you! Goodnight!"

Harrisson had blown a kiss from his fingertips. Sylvia disappeared.

In a laboratory next door to the master's, Lygie Rod leaned over a microscope. Harrison saw her through a window in the partition wall. He tapped it lightly, and the young woman raised her masked face.

"Still at work!" Harrisson exclaimed. "You won't be demanding a one-hour day, like our friends the domestic functionaries and the transport workers…"

Lygie emerged into the corridor and took off her mask. They talked about the new discovery. The young woman's calm voice became slightly more animated; on her lips, the harsh consonants of technical terms took on an unaccustomed softness.

"This tumultuous protoplasm," she said, "is quite something…magnificent and crazy! A crazy thing…"

"And perhaps a terrible thing," Harrisson added.

"Perhaps terrible…yes."

They were momentarily thoughtful; then Lygie asked: "You're going to publish a paper, of course?"

"No…not immediately, at any rate. I have anxieties. The Academy will publish without sufficient examination. Let's wait until after the centenary celebrations. Afterwards, we'll consider it, and we'll see…"

"Not everyone has your scruples," Lygie observed. "I was listening to the General News a little while ago. Lahorie's cousin, Roume, the geophysicist, has stirred up a lot of noise with his claim to have discovered a tertiary civilization far superior to human civilization. According to Roume, the Earth must have been inhabited for hundreds of thousands of years by beings endowed with immense knowledge, whom our distance ancestors would have served as domestic animals."

"Very good!" said Harrison. "There'll be no lack of subjects for discussion at the centenary congress. In that regard, Lygie, given that you pay attention to the press and are up to date with the news, can you tell me whether the program has been finalized? Someone was asking me just now. Will there be a dance performance? I'd like it if there were dancing…"

Lygie turned her head away. Her left hand leaned on the wall.

"I don't have any information about that," she replied, "but dancing seems to me, in fact, to be inevitable."

Harrisson was surprised by her ironic tone. He also noticed the sudden pallor of her face and the trembling of her mutilated hand.

II. The Interrupted Fête

The Minister of Public Festivities had issued orders to ensure fine weather between the principal lines framing 1.47. The state of the upper atmosphere had, in any case rendered the task of the meteorological contractors easy; a few artificial storms inside the quadrilateral, a little moderate turbulence at the angles, and a stable regime was established for at least forty-eight hours.

Early in the morning, the police occupied the principal surveillance posts, and the influx of delegates soon began. They came from the four corners of the world—not only scientists by artists, students, workers, agriculturalists, legislators and engineers: people of all kinds and all races.

One of the first to arrive was a young groom delegated by the navigation personnel of parallel aerial transport. He was taken to see Averine. After him came two old fishermen from Sakhalin and two students from a Mongol faculty of experimental psychology. In the morning, numerous officials got off the aerial express. A huge winged aerobus made of golden sheet metal circled for some time before landing; it brought Lahorie with his court of perverse young lyric poets and unbalanced pretty women.

All day long the sky was furrowed by aircraft. Excursionists made detours to salute 1.47 as they passed by. Some were attracted by curiosity, others by snobbery. Many were content to fly over the region slowly; at points designated by the police they let fall a rain of enormous flowers, which descended gently, suspended from parachutes sparkling with artificial gems. The travelers who wanted to land had to make a broad circuit and form a queue behind a guide, who took them to garages set up for the occasion. Fearful that his arrival might pass unperceived, Roume, the vainest of scientists, cut through the curtain of agents and fell from the clouds like a shell in a luxurious apparatus of the latest model. Immediately pulled over by two police vehicles, he made as much racket as was necessary to attract all attention to him.

Ladies were very numerous. Emerging from their hooded aircraft, rich Fuegian, Canadian and Swedish women quickly took refuge in the shade, or cast off their furs and opened light metallic umbrellas. Aristocratic ladies from Colombia and Indo-China, by contrast, sought out the sun and drew sumptuous shawls garnished with heat-producing radioactive filaments tight around their shoulders.

Some local residents came on foot. Modern railways no longer served to transport passengers, but the roads—beautiful roads with broad vitrified causeways—were still very busy. Nonchalant vehicles, whose speed rarely exceeded a hundred meters a second, still had their partisans among dreamers, invalids and people subject to vertigo.

A few young students even arrived at 1.47 mounted on horseback, wearing antique costumes with large shiny helmets like barbaric firemen, braided woolen jackets and heavy boots in natural leather. They were armed with carbines with nitrogenous powder cartridges and long raw steel sabers hung from their saddles. The crowd packed their route and cheered them; a few wanton women threw artificial flowers at them.

Considerable police forces had been deployed in the area. They suspected, in fact, that the aerial transport workers, whose recent claim for a one-hour day had been rejected, might do something. Supported by the latitudinal residents—domestic personnel, cinetelephonists, meteorologists, vitrifiers and power-station workers—the transport workers were opposed by the majority of agriculturalists, building workers and distributors; which is to say, almost all of the meridianist population. It would have been possible to satisfy their demand, but the reform would have upset a host of individuals and would inevitably have provoked other claims.

Furthermore the transport workless had spoiled their cause by making awkward and annoying secondary claims. With a spurious arrogance, they had demanded front-row seats at public solemnities, and wanted to require humiliating gestures of respect from travelers. The Supreme Council, recognizing that as detestable status pride, had vetoed it—and even if travelers had, in fact, been obliged to show humble deference, the law, at the very least would not have imposed sanctions on any failure of usage.

Thus, tempers remained overheated, all the more so because general elections were imminent. A workers' strike had just broken out, and it was feared in high places that the leaders might, by means of some absurd demonstration, disturb the serenity of the celebrations held in honor of Averine—celebrations that, thanks to the cinetelephone, the entire world would be able to watch.

The central authority had, therefore, taken its precautions. Airborne brigades equipped with rapid aircraft with independent engines were mounting incessant patrols high in the air. The zones of force were tightly guarded; the neighboring airport had been occupied.

In accordance with Averine's wishes, the organizers had maintained the strictest simplicity. In less than two days, employees of the temporary construction industry had erected vast metallic buildings in a meadow whose soil had been vitrified in advance.

The Congress opened at one o'clock in the afternoon, under the presidency of the Academic High Chancellor, representing the Supreme Power. Averine was on elevated platform; around him were his family and friends, a few students and the young groom from the aerial express, who scanned the audience with a bold and cheerful gaze. A thousand people had been accommodated in the hall.

A bell was rung. Immediately, all the members of the audience stood up and silence fell. At the same time, everyone in the entire world prepared to celebrate Averine; the presidents of ten thousand secondary assemblies opened sessions.

The police cinetelephonist began unmasking a battery of universal receivers installed at the top of the hall. At first, a kind of distant murmur was heard; one might have taken it for the countless rustlings of a forest beneath the thousand gusts of the wind. Slowly, the policeman turned the little wheel controlling the volume, and the noise grew as he did so; it was soon a hubbub of overlapping and discordant voices, but still distant and muffled. Finally, an immense clamor fell from the metallic vault. From all points of the globe, acclamations flew toward 1.47.

"Averine! Hurrah for Averine! Glory to Averine! Glory! Glory!"

The old man rose to his feet; upright, in a long white quasi-monastic costume, he appeared to millions of spectators. Immediately, the clamor changed.

"Let the sage speak! Let him speak to us!"

With an abrupt click, the policeman closed the volume control—and in the expectant silence, the grand old man spoke with simplicity to the peoples of the world.

"Why is your amity directed toward me? What have I done to deserve it? I tell you this: I don't know what I've done to deserve your amity. It's not certain that my work is good. At this moment, in truth, I'm not sure about that. I wonder what fruits the tree that I've planted will bear...and I'm anxious. You, who will live on the Earth after me, be prudent! Don't pick dangerous fruits without taking precautions. Be happy, with prudence! Be scientists, with prudence! Be just, with prudence! Against evil, fight with prudence! Don't strike the malevolent, disarm them. Be able to forgive; be able to suffer. There's no longer any certainty in my eyes but one, which is love. There's no virtue but love. There's no miracle but love. Love is the great security!"

A long ovation burst out in the hall; outside, the curious also applauded loudly, and dominating all of it was the immense acclamation of the distant auditors:

"Glory to Averine! Glory! Glory!"

When silence had been reestablished, a delegate from the Academy of Sciences summarized the master's works. He read his speech—an official speech which addressed the masses rather that the scholarly elites. Avoiding technical terms, he attempted to explain, in everyday language, by means of analogies and familiar comparisons, the strange novelty of Averine's work. He showed that the work opened previously forbidden horizons to human hope. Already, discoveries were succeeding one another with surprising rapidity, but those that had been made so far seemed trivial by comparison with those that would be made soon. All of that, they owed to

Averine—and the orator described the private life of the man who was entering immortality while alive, the simplest of the simple, the most modest of the modest, as great in heart as he was in mind.

The applause of the crowds saluted the speech. Then the session was suspended and Averine withdrew.

When it resumed, the session immediately seemed a trifle stormy. The Chancellor-President, in a brief speech, called for calm, reminding the delegates of character of the meeting and asking them not to forget that they were speaking and acting before the eyes of the entire world.

A philosopher adhering to old doctrines was the first to mount the podium. In his view, one could not honor Averine better than by following his advice. Had not the Master said: *love one another...forgive...don't strike the wicked*? He had said, above all, *be prudent...don't thoughtlessly pick fruit that might be poisonous*. It was important that humankind was ever more deeply penetrated by these essential truths. The lesson, very general, was for the scientists, but it also applied to politics and all the human groups who claims were tending to take on a bitter and urgent tone.

A meteorologist delegate replied straight away. He was an Asiatic from Petchili. He smiled as he spoke, without making the slightest gesture. Immediately, however, he shocked the assembly. He brought Averine the salute of the oppressed. No one gave the old doctrine of love a more sincere adherence than him—but, having taken that precaution, he declared without beating around the bush that justice was the highest reality of moral order. As long as the desire for justice did not exist in all human beings, as long as the light of day illuminated glaring inequalities, it was vain to talk about love. The orator did not cite any of these glaring inequalities; he stuck to vague and general terms, centuries-old clichés—but his voice carried, dry and contusive.

When he descended from the podium, a confused clamor emerged from the receivers. Exclamations were heard, the stamping of feet and shrill whistle-blasts. Then, as if in response to an agreed signal, furious applause drowned out everything, and a long cry sprang forth, uttered by millions of throats:

"Justice for all! Justice!"

At a sign from the president, the cinetelephonist closed the volume control again. In the hall, tempers were getting heated; a few delegates got up and made for the exit. Calm, however, was gradually reestablished. An agriculturalist spoke, and after him a power-station engineer. Their speeches did not lend themselves to controversy; they were merely explanations of the considerable progress that was owed to Averine in the material, practical and immediate order of things.

Roume followed them at the podium. He was a scientist of quality, but of overweening vanity. He seemed to want to approach the question from a philosophical direction, but by means of slippery and insidious detours he contrived to talk purely and simply about his own work, describing his latest resounding discovery: the existence of antediluvian superhumans, who had attained a prodigious state of civilization, whose race had disappeared completely at the beginning of the Tertiary Era,

Roume's example was contagious. Other scientists were equally concerned to make known to the entire world their successes, their hopes and their glory. One of them, whose theories had provoked some hilarity, appealed to Harrisson for support. All eyes turned toward Averine's favorite pupil, and all voices were soon appealing to him. They were astonished not to have heard from him; no one had more right than he had to speak on such an occasion.

Harrisson had not expected to get involved, but he yielded to the wishes of the assembly. His speech was not at all what the scientists expected of him. To general surprise, the audacious Harrisson, Harrisson the creator, only preached humility and prudence. *I don't know whether my work is good*, the master had said. All scientists could say the same. A scientific discovery, no matter how beautiful or important it might be, was not a good in itself. Roume's discovery—about which nothing, for the moment, permitted doubt—strongly reinforced that thesis. A terrible warning had risen from the night of time. That Tertiary civilization, so completely obliterated that it had required the most subtle resources of modern science to discover a few feeble traces of it, had very probably annihilated itself. Everything tended to suggest that those ancient masters of the Earth had met a brutal, instantaneous end, a catastrophic vanishment, and not the slow natural regression of a species that had reached the limit of its development. Humankind might disappear in the same fashion; old age did not threaten it in the least, but accident did.

Harrison emphasized the danger—a thousand times greater than before—of wretched ethnic or corporate rivalries. Humankind was too powerfully-armed to play such hazardous games again.

On the other hand, science, the sovereign of the world, ought to be considered as such. Far from demanding special rights for scientists, Harrisson wanted to see them subjected to a severe discipline. No laboratory, no research institute should escape public control. No discovery should any longer be announced before competent services had studied its potential repercussions. A new organization needed to be found: an organization that would probably be complicated, but which was imposed by urgent necessity.

Harrisson's speech did not excite any enthusiasm. There were murmurs in the hall. The company of scientists remained cold; many thought that their celebrated colleague was selling short the liberty of research, the primal condition of success. Most of the other delegates were hesitant.

Sensitive to the confused reactions of crowds, the poet Lahorie understood that an opportunity had presented itself to destroy the popularity of a significant adversary, a detested rival. He was prompt to seize it.

He began by reading, in a grave voice, a long poem in honor of Averine; then, in a religious silence, he improvised one of his finest harangues, before the eyes of the world. His voice, hesitant at first, blossomed and became thunderous; it was fraught, impetuous, pathetic. He described the slow ascent of humankind toward an ideal of liberty, justice and beauty. Everything that had been acquired since the beginning of the ages was owed to imprudent courage, to divine improvidence and uncalculating heroism.

He vituperated against the recent centuries that had seen the triumph of a limited utilitarianism. During that epoch of tedious wellbeing and moral apathy, pessimism and cowardice, people had never known the fresh joy of living. Now, thanks to the discoveries of Averine, who had enlightened the new world with a radiant dawn, a salutary reaction was taking place. In spite of the objurgations of a blind and exhausted philosophy, people were instinctively rediscovering the strong essential virtues that had led the species from ancestral animality to its present supremacy. Souls emerging from their artificial and unhealthy lethargy were resuming their thrust toward the summits, boldly and dangerously, in a dazzle of light and joy.

The formidable ovation of the distant auditors saluted Lahorie's speech. The breath of crowds swept forth like a tempest: "Glory to Averine! Glory to Lahorie! Justice and liberty! Justice! Justice!"

The poet descended from the podium, his heart swollen with pride. Brushing aside with a noble gesture the delegates who wanted to bear him aloft in triumph, he headed slowly, with the gravity of an idol, toward the group of his young disciples.

The rumor of the crowds, meanwhile, died away; one clear sentence, doubtless originating from a nearby transmitter, emerged from the receivers.

"That imbecile's at least ten centuries behind the times!"

Harrisson recognized the voice of Lygie Rod. Lahorie heard it too, and it spoiled the joy of his triumph.

At eight o'clock in the evening the banquet brought together five hundred guests under the presidency of the Monitress General of Games and Festivals.

Before the meal, according to custom, the president, accompanied by her maids of honor, went to the kitchens and offered bread and wine on a golden platter to the gourmet-in-chief, the head of the domestic staff. Houses like Averine's, in which the guests really served the domestic functionaries, were, in fact, very rare; the latter usually had to be content with a symbolic offering. At public feasts, there was always a brief propitiatory ceremony.

The gourmet-in-chief broke the bread and raised the heavy goblet sparkling with gems to his lips. Then he rang a silvery bell three times; in response to that signal, the guests took their seats.

There were three large metallic tables, softly and variable luminous. A few domestic functionaries supervised the service at a distance by means of a small portable keyboard. Above the tables sparkled a complicated machinery; the automatic servers traveled incessantly back and forth along rigid slipways; prehensile apparatus ornamented with flowers descended silently before each guest, depositing a fruit, cutlery and a glass, and rose up again, carrying the empty plates. Various liquids flowed from silver fountains.

The tables were laden with enormous fruits and rare flowers. Horticulturalists had presented their most recent creations: gigantic flowers and monstrous hybrids, with marvelously delicate or exotic coloration. American enthusiasts had succeeded in producing astonishing ultra-rapid and ephemeral blossoms. Before the guests' eyes, buds grew and erupted; in a matter of minutes, madly exuberant corollas were seen, palpitating, which soon paled and bent over in order to die.

The first course was a pink one: the lights of the phosphorescent ramps were pink, as were the muted luminosity of the tables, the glasses, the myrtle wine, and the bunches of flowers. A light rustic music fell like crystalline rain, and the sound of voices was light too, bell-like and clear. The guests made contact. All races and all conditions were represented there. The masculine costumes presented a remarkable diversity—a sign of the times. Half a century earlier, traveling costumes and ceremonial dress had scarcely varied from continent to continent; now, every people strove, on the contrary, toward specific types. The yellow men wore loose-fitting blouses with capacious sleeves, the black men brightly-colored tunics. The poet Lahorie, an Arab by origin, had draped himself in a huge burnoose of red artificial silk. Women did not escape worldwide fashion as easily as the men. A few of them, among the youth of the white race, risked long hair, but they all wore brocaded metallic dresses, high on the left side and leaving the right side naked to the waist—and all of them, similarly, had their foreheads and hair dyed dark green.

Hazard had placed Harrisson not far away from Lygie Rod. He was astonished to find her there, so hostile was she to gatherings of that sort; examining her surreptitiously, he was also astonished to see her animated and adorned like a socialite. To her right she had a rival of Harrisson's, the Japanese Takase, smiling and courteous; to her left, Roume. The latter was holding forth, and Lygie seemed to be taking a mischievous pleasure in feeding him cues, pushing his glory ever higher.

"Don't you think, Master, that your Tertiary superhumans can be conceived as the gods—or, at least the demigods—of legend? Perhaps they were pure spirits?"

"On the contrary, Mademoiselle, my work has proved that they were material beings endowed with a life analogous to ours…with, however, a few singularities that I propose to determine."

"In that case, Master, it's necessary to admit the catastrophic vanishment of which our colleague Harrisson spoke a little while ago."

Roume immediately riposted: "Our honorable colleague has merely reiterated a hypothesis that I formulated myself a long time ago. It's the first that springs to mind...but here are others—for example, that of a total emigration of the superhumans to another planet."

Discreet laughter was heard, but Lygie continued, imperturbably: "That might perhaps explain many things. Who would dare to swear that we are not still under the domination of those emigrants—that the absurd movements of our poor humanity are not directed at a distance by the insidious will of our former masters? Besides which, the tumultuous protoplasm studied by our colleagues Harrisson and Takase..."

Roume interrupted her. "I was the first," he said, "to bring to light the astral influences on artificial life. I'm still pursuing my research, so I can't say anything precise for the moment."

The musical accompaniment became more emphatic; the pink course as replaced by the green course. The tables were now emitting a glaucous glow; the light of the ramps seemed to be filtering through a curtain of young foliage. A bunch of pale green flowers had fallen from the ceiling. The fountains were pouring out emerald wines.

The murmur of voices covered the slight clicking of the serving apparatus and the sound of clinking crystal. The effect of exhilarating pills was already evident; bursts of troubled laughter suddenly rose up and broke off abruptly, or terminated in a kind of shrill plaint. Already drunk, an equivocal ephebe, Lahorie's companion, was shaken by irrepressible giggles.

Dances had been announced for the final violet course, but murmurs were heard against the organizers before the green service had finished. Numerous guests, belong to all social classes, wanted circus games. At the central banquet, the murmurs remained discreet, but loud demands coming from the distant banquets that were taking place at the same time emerged from the universal receivers.

The president yielded to the popular will. From her seat, she issued orders in various directions to the organizers of the games. To either side of the hall there was a vast cinetelegraphic screen on which every guest could easily follow the distant scenes with their eyes.

During the blue course, they watched a battle between panthers and mastiffs. That was happening in central Africa, thousands of leagues away, but one could nevertheless see the palpitation of ripped flesh, the somersaults of panting beasts and the streaming of blood. The howls of the dogs drowned out the savage chords of the accompanying music.

By the indigo light they followed the dangerous tricks of a troop of acrobats. One young trapeze-artist, almost a child, performed at a height of a thousand meters, suspended from a parachute. Then a celebrated Mexican tenor sang, in the midst of general indifference.

The atmosphere became heavy with violent perfumes. Staccato laughter increasingly dominated the sound of conversations. The exhilarant poison caused faces to grimace and made gesture discordant.

The appearance of a gigantic negro brought attention back to the screens.

"Orog! Orog! Long live Orog!"

The man came forward, his loins covered with an animal skin and a stone ax in his hand. Suddenly, a lion bounded in front of him.

The combat was unexpectedly rapid. The wild beast launched itself forward. As motionless as a bronze statue, Orog waited. The heavy flint smashed into the monstrous skull, and the lion fell on its side. Orog was on to it like lightning; the crack of vertebrae was heard. Laid low, with its back broken, the lion swiveled neverthe-less, and the man could not avoid its raised claw. The animal skin covering his loins was snatched away; blood ran from his somber thighs—but the certainty of victory multiplied his strength tenfold. The stone ax crushed the paws, laid the ribs bare and shattered the skull. Soon, the lion was no longer moving.

The acclamation of the crowds, muffled by the vol-ume control, rumbled like an earthquake. Orog stood over the vanquished beast. Completely nude and un-steady on his feet, he displayed his bloody breast and wounded limbs with proud laughter—and suddenly col-lapsed, face forwards, while the frantic clamors were redoubled.

At the principal banquet, as elsewhere, people had applauded noisily. The muted expression of a barbaric joy cracked the worldly varnish; eyes were shining; in-voluntary grimaces revealed the hypocrisy of blasé ex-pressions. Slow voluptuous laughter mingled with intox-icated outbursts of artificial gaiety. Wines flowed in abundance.

Immobile and scornful, the domestic employees or-dered the final course. The tables, with amethyst gleams, were covered with enormous violets. Other violets, very small and miraculously delicate by way of contrast, fell like odorous snow on to the shoulders of the guests.

Dances began to animate the screens. First, Sylvia appeared in the midst of her pupils. She led graceful evolutions, but with a slightly cold classical correctness.

Harrisson glanced covertly at Lygie; she was smil-ing ironically, her lips pursed.

After the ensemble, Sylvia appeared on her own, in her musical dances. Naked, she mimed the adventure of love in a harmonious room. It was her latest composition, which won her the applause of crowds as well as the admiration of connoisseurs. The artistry of the musician completed, in her, the artistry of the dancer. Each of her steps on the sonorous floor and each of the gestures of her superb body struck languorous and passionate chords.

This evening, however, the marvelous dance did not excite enthusiasm. After the violent games, the spectacle of art seemed insipid. Only the guests at the principal banquet offered polite applause. Sylvia disappeared, furious.

The distant banquets were completed in a hubbub punctuated by brutal clamors. Several times, the revolutionary anthem of the workers of the parallels was heard. Averine's birthday was turning into a political manifestation almost everywhere. At the principal banquet, however, appearances remained correct until the end.

At a signal from the gourmet-in-chief, white light was switched on. The guests left the room silently and in order, beneath the severe gaze of the domestic personnel.

Harrisson rejoined Averine on the terrace of 1.47. Lygie, who was already with the old man, could not suppress a gesture of astonishment on seeing the young scientist. Harrisson felt obliged to justify his presence, and replied to the inferred question in a low voice.

"Yes, it's true...I was to have left this evening...and yet, here I am, with you..."

The young woman, who as leaning on the balustrade, moved away slightly. Her speech was veiled with irony. "The evening began badly for you...it will end the same way."

"Indeed," Harrisson replied, "this will be a very bad evening for me if you speak to me in that tone, Lygie."

In the shadow, where she was, he could not make out her facial features very well. He saw her eyes widen, though, and divined that she was shaken by emotion, in the fearful expectation of joy. He, too, was choked by anguish then, and the conclusive words froze on his lips.

At thirty-five years of age, Harrisson had scarcely known anything but the fever of research, the slightly crude and prideful intoxication of an adventurous conquistador of thought. He had been greatly disturbed when he had discovered in Lygie, instead of fraternal sympathy or a cerebral amity, a more complex, profound and tender attachment.

He entered into the world of sentiment; he entered it awkwardly, as if regretfully, disorientated by the insufficiency, in that domain, of the stern habits of a logician.

Lygie was leaning on the balustrade, where her mutilated hand made a pale patch. Gazing at that hand, Harrisson remembered the circumstances of the accident, the young woman's tranquil courage. She had resumed her post in the laboratory long before the injury had healed.

For the first time, he appreciated at its true value the attentive and passionate aid that she had given to him since she had arrived at the Averine Institute.

I've been beside her for many long days, he thought, *without knowing her...and I didn't know myself any better*.

There was a rather long silence between them, and then Harrisson was only able to pronounce ordinary words.

"Wasn't it you, Lygie, who appreciated Lahorie's harangue so keenly? I thought I recognized the sound of your voice."

Lygie had recovered a little of her self-composure; she moved into the light and said: "Indeed, I appreciated it as it deserved. I was here, at this very spot, next to the Master. He was listening to Lahorie, whose speech pained him—and it was for the Master that I spoke. Unfortunately, I didn't take account of the transmitter, which was on…there, close at hand!"

They fell silent again, and then turned to Averine. The old man was in his armchair, in his usual spot. His eyes looked at the two young people tenderly, and his eyes cleared. He made a gesture as if to draw them together and murmured: "It's necessary to take the time to love, my children."

They looked at one another, and the same pallor flowed over their serious faces. In the silence, it seemed to them that the beating of their hearts must be discernible. Words were unnecessary…

Samuel and Flore appeared on the terrace and came to slip between them in order to see the nocturnal festivities. It was already late, and Harrisson said: "Aren't you going to bed, Master? This has been a tiring day for you."

"I don't feel tired," the old man replied. "A little sad, though…for it appears to me that the new humans lack wisdom. Anxiety is hollowing out its wound within me." He paused, then continued: "The weather's mild, though…and this corner of the world is beautiful, thanks to human industry. Let's rejoice, therefore, in our eyes and our souls."

With a slow gesture, he indicated the magical spectacle. The entire region was illuminated. The habitations aligned their resplendent gables; in the parks and gardens, along the roads, railways and aerial routes, millions of fires moved past one another. The light seemed to be welling up from the ground and flowing everywhere. The soft nocturnal breezes caused innumerable fluorescent feathers to bob and sway in the treetops. From one minute to the next, the spectacle varied infinitely. There were fires in eclipse, scintillations, geysers of gems, the sudden blooming of unreal flowers, and also placid gleams, slow metamorphoses, rainbow separations of the fingers of nonchalant fairies. And everywhere, there were exotic spectra of ephemeral colors: an immense, inconceivable fluttering, to which nothing natural could compare.

The sky was no less sumptuous and no less strange.

The zones displayed their walls of light there. From vast artificial clouds, brightly-colored elongated tresses wandered and floated. Finally, thousands of aircraft were traveling with all their lights on.

The guests of the central banquet and the curiosity-seekers had, in fact, reached the upper atmosphere. From the neighboring airport, public vehicles were rising up, carrying the delegates to distant countries. Young people, students, socialites and all those in possession of an apparatus with an independent engine were staying for the nocturnal festivities. Aircraft could be seen climbing toward the zenith at vertiginous speed, and letting themselves fall, playfully, streaking the sky like shooting stars.

Almost every apparatus was decorated, often with originality. Some had been rigged out in the form of boats, and were sailing smoothly, as if the wind alone were blowing in their sails. Fiery horses scaled the clouds, drawing chariots with sparkling wheels. A battle of luminous flowers began, directly above 1.47.

Police aircraft were watching over the festival, recognizable by their bright red stationary lights.

Throughout the sky there was a formidable scattering, a supernatural, hallucinatory confusion something too rich for human eyes, habituated for millennia to the simple and grave beauty of the hours of darkness.

Harrisson observed Averine's melancholy. "Master," he said, "it's thanks to you that humans can put on such a spectacle."

The old man replied: "Anxiety is wounding me..." He lowered his dazzled eyes and murmured timidly: "I'm dreaming...of the scintillation of stars in the profundity of abysms...the gentle royalty of the moon...the filtration of a thin shaft of light through sleepy foliage..."

Harrison suddenly leaned over the balustrade. He scrutinized the eastern horizon, where twenty aircraft flying in strict formation had just appeared, but which did not carry the red light of police vehicles. Lygie had noticed the new arrivals too; she unmasked the receivers on the terrace. Immediately, dominating the noise of the aerial fête, a revolutionary song burst forth, formidably amplified on transmission by powerful resonators.

Harrisson made a desolate gesture.

"Here come the party-poopers!" he said. "They'll end up spoiling their own cause. How dare they, at such a moment?"

The aircraft were approaching rapidly, dispersing beams of light from every porthole. The police could be seen assembling; a brigade set off to confront the newcomers. The latter went higher. The revolutionary song had ceased, but an impassioned cry filled the air:

"Justice! Justice!"

Large luminous banners were released by the aircraft and floated in the wind. Threatening inscriptions in enormous letters could be read thereon.

The one-hour day or death!

In Averine's century, justice must reign.
In Averine's century, power is in the hands of all.
We shall strike and we shall vanquish!
Beware of surprises!

Lygie closed the receivers—but the old man had heard the brutal refrain and could see, written in the sky, the arrogant folly of the adventure-seekers. A great sadness darkened his features; he put his hands over his face.

The police, however, had caught up with the strikers. They surrounded them, seeking to draw them away in order to force them to land outside the illuminated zone.

The police aircraft were, in fact, equipped with powerful interrupters, permitting them to slow down or stop independent engines at a distance. This time, however, the pursued aircraft did not obey, doubtless making use of some unfamiliar system of propulsion. Similar misadventures had happened quite often to the police since the recent discoveries of Averine's pupils.

Once again a banner was released, bearing the disquieting and mocking: *Beware of surprises.*

A second brigade of aircraft with red lights came to the rescue. The public watched, amused by the unexpected incident. The students, abandoning their games, steered toward the site of the encounter, entirely ready to jeer at the police and hinder their action.

Definitely powerless to force a landing, the police maneuvered, coming together in an opposed line, forming a close-range barrage. The strikers made a half-turn and made off. Suddenly, an aircraft peeled off from their group and, disdaining all pretence, plunged straight ahead at high speed. There was a certain flutter in the police line; prudently, the aircraft in the center moved aside. The striker passed through.

Unfortunately a brigadier of terrible enthusiasm was in command there. He was slightly behind and above the barrage of agents. Perceiving the gap, he let himself fall into it with meteoric speed. The striker tried to slow down and avoid him, but it was too late. The two aircraft collided, annihilating one another in the same explosion. Flaming debris fell into the valley.

The drama had been so unexpected and so rapid that many of the spectators did not understand what had happened at first, and believed it to be an ordinary accident—but the strikers' resonators resounded with frantic cries:

"Murderers!"

"Murderers!"

"Vengeance!"

For their part, the police, losing all self-control, took aim with their missile-launchers. That was a grave threat, of which they rarely made use. A single projectile could not only pulverize any apparatus it touched directly, but, if it exploded in the midst of a group, could throw the engineers out of kilter and blow them all up.

Surprised, the strikers gave up; they disappeared toward the east, flying at top speed.

Gently swaying in the wind, one last banner continued to float: *Beware of surprises!* The police destroyed it.

The drama, rapid and brutal, and left an anguish in every heart—an anguish that increased from one moment to the next, by virtue of the furious clamor that was now coming from the four corners of the horizon, which resounded from all the receivers:

"Vengeance! Vengeance!"

The battle of the flowers had ceased. The aircraft returned to the festival rigging and prepared to leave. A heavily-laden express was already rising up from the airport. The last officials and the numerous idlers directed their machines toward the bright heights of the neighboring public zone.

Abruptly, that light went out! And all the nebulae of the atmosphere and lights playing on the surface of the earth went out too. A sudden darkness descended upon the region; the only lights still shining were those of aircraft with independent engines. The stars and the slender crescent of the moon were visible.

Harrisson had precipitated himself toward the receivers. They were no longer working.

The striking workers, by some unknown method, had just taken action against the central power-station, thus paralyzing a entire region—an action without precedent, whose success could only be explained by accomplices highly-placed in the scientific world.

Cries of distress rang out in the air. The overloaded express fell, in spite of its emergency motors. A hundred meters from the ground, it recovered slightly, but came to earth nevertheless among the trees of a park, where several huts were smashed. The private machines engaged in the public zone made emergency landing simultaneously in the dark countryside. The others remained in the air, heading for the heights in order to find reference-points. The police aircraft circled dazedly, projecting powerful beams of red light at random, which only added to the confusion.

Following a plan doubtless prepared far in advance, the meteorological workers, making common cause with the strikers, unleashed bad weather. A violent wind began to blow; stormy clouds formed on the spot, growing with astonishing rapidity. The stars disappeared, and the most powerful searchlights were soon stifled by thick mists. Every extinct nebula became the center of a formidable whirlwind. On the round, roofs were torn off and trees broken, large branches borne away like wisps of straw. The temporary buildings of the Congress fell apart noisily.

Aircraft were no longer cleaving the sky; the most rapid had fled, light pleasure-craft with weak engines having been transported long distances or forced into hard landings.

Natural lightning striped the clouds. A police aircraft that as still in the sir was struck; a huge flame was seen, and then the darkness closed in again. The night was as black as ink.

Some distance from 1.47, enormous hailstones bombarded the earth, slashing the trees and denting the thin metal roofs of houses.

In the darkness, Samuel and Flore huddled together and uttered cries of fright.

Harrisson and Lygie went to Averine.

"Master," said Harrisson, "it would be prudent to leave this place."

The old man did not reply. Tipped back against the back of his chair, his head was a pale patch.

Averine was dead.

Thunder filled the sky with its puerile and barbaric violence.

III. A Political Trial

The strikers' assault only claimed twenty victims, but political passions, heated by the approach of general elections, gave the affair an enormous resonance.

Almost all the victims belonged to the so-called privileged classes; they were agriculturalists, engineers, legislators and important functionaries. Indignation was great among the meridian populations.

For their part, the parallelists made accusations of police brutality, complained of *agents provocateurs* at the Ministry of Fêtes, and took the responsibility all the way to the Supreme Council, who, not content to reject the justified demands of the workers, had sought to bully them by refusing them the right to demonstrate.

In each party, a few wise men tried in vain to restore the affair to its veritable proportions. No one listened to them; in fact, they were vilified. The floor was held by the disaffected and those fishing in troubled waters. The cinetelephone carried the speeches of the hotheads into the isolated houses of the secondary networks. Uninterrupted pulsations of violence shook humankind, awakening dormant instincts, disequilibrating defenseless minds and troubling the best.

Brawls broke out; they were very frequent at exchange stations and public vehicles between operators and passengers, the latter refusing the former manifest gestures of respect, and multiplying demands.

The sudden death of Averine, caused by the desolating spectacle of civil discord, was exploited by everyone. Each party claimed the glorious cadaver for itself. Each party, in addition, protested against oppression and talked about nothing but justice. The evident sincerity of the greater number rendered the situation disquieting.

Meanwhile, the Supreme Council remained silent; prudently, it was content to observe, relying on the imminent elections to pacify the tempest again.

The trial of the strikers was followed with passionate attention, but was conducted no less regularly for that, according to the forms prescribed by worldwide legislation.

On the day after the assault, fifteen transport employees had been arrested, but their accomplices in meteorology and the laboratories escaped the initial investigation. The accused were locked up in a temporary prison not far from 1.47, on the scene of the crime. Numerous police forces were on alert and all the power-stations in the region closely watched.

As soon as the investigation began, the accused provoked an incident; subject to the political regime, they appealed to common law.[10] Their demand was rejected. Although anticipated and entirely regular, that first legal decision provoked a lively agitation among the people of the parallels.

The political regime was not, in fact, without grave inconveniences for the accused. A vulgar murderer could hope to benefit from a disdainful pity. Against the isolated and banal crime, society reacts without brutality; it crushes the monstrous but individual, testimony of a return to a barbarism too distant to be veritably contagious,

---

[10] I have translated these terms directly, although they sound slightly awkward and "common law" has a different significance in English from the one intended; the distinction is presumably an echo of the contemporary distinction between criminal and civil law.

without hatred. By contrast, it puts itself violently on the defensive against political crimes with hazardous repercussions.

Scientific civilization had bound all humans together with the threads of a solidarity so complex, interests were so entangled, and disorder could lead to such catastrophes, that the harsh legislators of the first century had not hesitated to arm society strongly against frenetic trouble-makers.

Whereas the accused of common law benefited from a rather benign regime, receiving General News from outside and even communicating, under certain conditions, with their families, political prisoners were isolated and forbidden communication. The prosecution could, in addition, employ in their respect subtle and forceful procedures that were, in principle, not entirely unlike of the torture of the barbaric ages.

Thus, an expert psychologist was immediately appended to the examining magistrate in charge of the investigation of the strikers. Since the third century, psychology had, in fact, been an experimental science; delicate apparatus permitted mental introspection, even revealing the mysterious workings of the unconscious.

An initial summary examination, only differing from the examinations of ancient psychiatrists in the precision of the results, enabled the accused to be sorted into three categories. Two of them produced a high curve on the metal oscillator, ten were classed in the median range and three were classed as weak. The last group immediately passed into the regime of common law, and a fortnight later, and ordinary tribunal sentenced them to light punishments.

For the others, the process was much longer. No meteorologist had yet been caught, so the examining magistrate's first task was the search for accomplices. Direct interrogation having yielded nothing, the expert intervened. He soon discovered reticence and lies in one of the accused with a high curve. While the others only seemed to have been agents of execution, this one assumed the appearance of the leader. The investigation concentrated on his efforts, but the man was capable of defending himself; nothing could be extracted from him by ordinary methods.

Then he fell prey to the psychologist.

For a long day, in the changing light of a laboratory, among strange instruments, he was subjected to complicated ordeals. He went rapidly through the full range of hypnotic states; he experienced provoked hallucination, vertigo, terror, mad gaiety, esthetic exaltation and numerous temporary neuroses. During each test, special apparatus registered the totality of his psychic reactions. At the end of the day, the expert had in hand a series of graphics permitting the precise definition of the subject's mental characteristics.

The man having refused once again to identify his accomplices voluntarily, the magistrate, after the customary summations, solemnly announced that musical questioning would be applied the following day, at noon, local time, in the usual form. Two minutes later, vehement protests from all points of the globe emerged from the receivers.

Unlike the preliminary ordeals, musical questioning was applied in public; it could be followed and monitored by everyone via cinetelephonic screens.

At the appointed hour, the accused was taken to the judiciary psychology laboratory, where he was immobilized under a bell of isolating mesh, impermeable to psychic waves coming from outside. There were only a small number of curiosity-seekers at the laboratory; two policemen sufficed to keep them at a safe distance. On the other hand, thousand of distant spectators were following the scene passionately. In order to ensure perfect transmission, bright artificial light was added to the daylight illuminating the laboratory.

The preparations only lasted five minutes, the time to tune the psychological inductors to the metal helmet with which the accused was coiffed. As soon as synchronicity was established, the control apparatus, a kind of ultra-sensitive microphone, emitted a continuous sound of slightly variable intensity, similar to the buzz of an active beehive, considerably amplified. For some accused, resistant to its influence, that synchronicity did not last long, but the slightest discord between the brain of the subject and the inductors was translated into characteristic grating and crackling sounds. Immediately, the apparatus was retuned. Any possibility of deception or error was thus removed, and the results of the musical questioning were unarguable.

The accused, profiting from his last moments of mental liberty, hurled his protest in the face of the world; he railed, not without eloquence, against the pitiless procedures of modern torturers, the burglars of consciousness.

The imperturbable psychologist, however, leaned over his apparatus. With each of his gestures, economical and precise, the orator's words became less certain. Soon, as the microphone began to hum, they were no more than an incoherent stammer. A few words could still be heard: "justice…liberty…torturers…pirates…" but then the microphone alone uttered its monotonous song. His consciousness completely besieged, the man smiled vaguely; his eyes were haggard.

Then the examining magistrate asked a few questions—questions that were not very insidious; mere stimuli to relax the mental automatism.

Immediately, the confession flowed out like an avalanche.

In a strange voice, sometimes trembling with anger, sometimes punctuated with dolorous bursts of laughter, like the voice of a dreamer talking in his sleep, the man revealed all the circumstances of the assault.

The accused identified himself as the organizer of the demonstration that had preceded the assault. On his orders, a striker had driven straight at the police blockade. On his orders, similarly, the power-stations had been switched off. Finally, at a signal from him, the meteorologists had taken action.

He named his principal accomplices: six meteorologists, two engineers—one of them well-known, the leader of a parallelist group in the World Parliament—and finally, a young physicist, a former collaborator of Harrisson.

Arrest warrants were immediately issued.

The accused had stopped speaking. With a flick of a switch, the psychologist plunged him into a reparative sleep, and two policeman carried the unconscious man back to the prison.

The police had no difficulty arresting the guilty physicist and the two engineers. The parliamentarian engineer was arrested in the Chamber in mid-session. His mandate, far from conferring immunity upon him, exposed him to serious punishment, but his complicity was indirect. He did not strive desperately to get himself out of trouble, and even saw his political support consolidated.

The arrest of the meteorologists was much more difficult. As soon as the magistrate's decision announcing the musical questioning was announced, they had taken flight. Two of them were arrested in southern Africa, aboard a public aerobus on a secondary network. Another had taken refuge in a hospital for domestic personnel, a somnarium, where he was indulging in the luxury of long siestas; he was denounced by a nurse. The remaining three, two men and a woman, had to be pursued for a long through the crowded skies.

A week after the last arrests, the affair came to trial. A long session was devoted to the official publication of the charge sheet: a considerable document, which a loud-hailer made known to the entire world.

The defense had summoned fifty witnesses belonging to all classes of society. The majority knew nothing about the outrage—or, at least, nothing more than had been supplied by the General News—but each witness came to make a sentimental plea on behalf of one or other of the accused. Some made political speeches that had no relevance to the trial.

One vainglorious and disreputable journalist, an electoral agent of the parallelist party, dared to make a direct apology for revolutionary violence. He was arrested. The political leaders of the parallelists immediately went into action. Parallelist strikes broke out simultaneously, and for twenty-four hours held over the world the threat of a collective resignation of meteorological and transport workers.

To tell the truth, for the moment it was nothing but a bluff, but the symptom was nevertheless disturbing. The Supreme Council, abandoning its strategy of temporization, imposed its authority with an almost-forgotten rudeness. There was an unexpected upheaval of social defense. The active police forces were issued with new weapons and stern instructions; the reserve forces were to be ready to intervene at the first appeal. Finally, a rigorous censorship would filter all the communications of the General News.

Surprised by this energetic resistance, the agitators lowered their flag. There were tremors of anger among the sincere crowds, but minds numbed by five centuries of rough discipline were not yet ripe for great adventures. Once again, superior prudence was imposed, suppressing discordant passions, consolidating and unifying them.

The trial continued in due legal form. The defense made skillful use of elevated testimony. It called philosophers imbued with modern ideas, men whose good faith could not be called into doubt. In a tone of great moderation, it constructed a pitiless critique of the organization of the world. After their intervention, news and unexpected support rallied to the defense. The poet Lahorie demanded to be heard.

Lahorie had fallen back under the yoke of the dancer Sylvia. The latter, cruelly wounded by Harrisson's scorn, had sworn to exact vengeance, and of that vengeance the conceited poet was to be the docile instrument. He therefore presented himself in person before the tribunal in order to bring the accused physicist the testimony of his sympathy. What chain of circumstances had brought the young scientist before the judges today? His first and greatest crime, Lahorie said—unpardonable in the eyes of some—had been to be ranked among the best pupils of Averine. His youthful enthusiasm, his nascent renown and his success had caused resentment; a colleague, a great hoarder of treasures who edified his own glory with the work of others, had had him expelled

85

from the Etheric Institute. Embittered, only able to work in difficult circumstances, the young scientist had turned to the people. If there was a guilty physicist in this affair, he was not before the judges; it was necessary to seek him among the privileged, among the pontiffs of official science...

The attack was direct, naïve and absurd. However, Lahorie was allowed to speak until the end. The celebrated poet could not be treated in the same cavalier fashion as some unknown pontificator. Whatever he said, in any case, his eloquent speech stirred the immense audience; even his enemies were subject to his charm.

The prosecution riposted by calling Harrisson. The latter spoke via the cinetelephone, without leaving the laboratory where he was working alongside Lygie. In a few simple sentences he exonerated himself.

Then, a question from the defense led him to ask the indulgence of the tribunal for the accused, especially for the physicist, no reportage having anticipated, in fact, any sanction against the initial fault of the latter—and Harrisson was gradually drawn to deplore the absence of the organization of scientific work. Once again, with all the force of increased conviction, he sounded the cry of alarm.

His deposition—which was, in principle, only intended to respond to a precise question—thus took on a vaster significance. It had an unexpected resonance, arousing more protests than applause elsewhere. Many groups, accustomed to the renewed individualist theories of antiquity, accused Harrisson of reactionary pessimism. However, even among the people, the opinion of such a justly-celebrated scientist could not be held to be negligible. Heated arguments broke out between partisans of Lahorie and partisans of Harrisson. The former having put forward his candidacy for the World Parliament in view of the imminent vote, Harrisson thus found himself, in spite of his wishes, shoved into the political arena.

The trial concluded in a stormy atmosphere.

The speeches of the advocates were unusually violent. The pitiless censorship of the General News aggravated opinion and was counterproductive. Strange rumors propagated regardless; the slightest of them grew immeasurably as it circulated around the planet.

Anonymous threats rained down on the jurors. One of them, suspected of hostility with regard to the accused, was attacked in an even more cowardly manner; his two children disappeared, taken hostage and sequestered while the verdict was awaited.

Once again, this violence marred the cause of the accused. The sentence was passed, pitilessly. It was death for the four principal guilty parties, and temporary internment in an establishment for psychic correction for the others.

The latter punishment seemed to some people to be more cruel than death. Delivered to specialist psychiatrists, the condemned were submitted for several months to a progressive treatment that gradually disaggregated their personality. The will founded in the early days; then, one after another, all the faculties of rationality; finally, memory was also obliterated. The patients fell into a profound mental lethargy, a slow state of life comparable, in the confusion of reflexes, to uterine life. Once they were at that point, their personalities were rebuilt—but that second part of the treatment, much less rapid than the first, was also much less efficacious and less sure, usually only yielding pitiful results. The psychic life thus reawakened remained summary, and did not always reach even the level of superior animality. The poor creatures were set free, forever inoffensive, undoubtedly, but no longer having anything but the appearance of humanity, and it was often necessary to hospitalize them.

The severity of the judgment caused real ill-feeling throughout the world. It appeared to benevolent minds, otherwise little inclined to tolerate the arrogance of the strikers and their partisans, to be excessive.

Vanquished, the strikers' partisans entered a routine appeal, and threw all their weight into the electoral battle.

IV. Harrisson's Defeat

Nothing was more alien to Harrison than political ambition. Even before winning renown, when he was only a young, completely unknown physicist, he had put his research work above everything, and would have preferred the ingrate labor of a laboratory assistant to the brilliant and hectic life of a leader of men. Between a seat on the Supreme Council and the humble metal stool on to which he let himself fall in front of his experimental bench, when fatigue exhausted his limbs, he would not have hesitated for a second.

It was, therefore, with a veritable annoyance that he found himself solicited by countless unknown individuals from all over the world, who begged him publicly to seek a mandate to the World Parliament. At every electoral period, certain candidates, and not the least, found themselves thus designated by the popular voice, independent of and even in opposition to their own will. It was a sort of preparatory vote in which the people chose, without consulting them, those most worthy.

It was not customary, in such cases for the persons selected by a significant mass of electors not to take their chance. To refuse the mandate—or, rather, to refuse the battle—was considered to be an admission of egotism and cowardice, and resulted in the loss of the right to vote for a period of ten years.

Even so, Harrisson hesitated. He wanted for scientists, not the agitations of politics, but the more effective role of technical advisors with regard to the supreme power. Furthermore, Harrisson was, at that moment, occupied in passionate research, gripped by a fever of curiosity and endeavor, as in the best years of his career. Finally, he had Lygie, the forceful maid with the luminous brain and the pure heart. The two young people worked side by side, enveloped by sovereign peace; their love, scarcely expressed, ripened like the rarest fruit in the discreet shade of their life—and Harrison was slightly fearful of the brutal glare of broad daylight.

It was, however, because of Lygie that, in a moment of indignation and anger, he came to an abrupt decision.

Sylvia was silently pursuing her vengeance from afar. The sure instinct of a woman scorned guided her thrusts toward Lygie. Thanks to her, for some time, covert slanders had been circulating in the scientific world. Lahorie, in his harangues and even in her verses, made transparent allusions to her. Finally, one evening, as Harrisson and Lygie were together in the library, listening to the News by cinetelephone, and abominable anonymous echo reached them. An unknown voice, coming from an untraceable station, told the story of a scientist, the director of a famous Institute, a man both very pretentious and very naïve, who had allowed himself to be ensnared by a female laboratory technician, a joyful courtesan in her early youth, whose self-interested favors had enchanted a number of libidinous old men.

Harrisson was so upset that he did not even think, at first, of turning down the volume, and he had the agony of listening to the outbursts of ironic laughter that greeted the filthy slander in the distance.

He looked at Lygie. The young woman had not budged. In her pale, desolate face, nothing was any longer alive but her eyes, full of distress. Harrisson went to her and took her small trembling hands.

"Lygie!" he murmured. "Lygie!"

He drew the young woman toward him and wrapped his arms around her in a protective gesture—but the insulting laughter could still be heard in the distance.

He turned round and smashed the apparatus with furious blows. And in his wrath, he struck out at random, interrupting all communication with the public zones. Immediately, silence fell and all the lights went out.

Harrisson drew Lygie to the window, open to the mild and perfumed night—and their betrothal was finally sealed, while the familiar nightingale sang in the midst of the sleeping garden, as strange in the moonlight as in the earliest ages of the world.

The next day, Harrison announced, via the General News, his imminent marriage to Lygie Rod, correspondent of the Academies of Physics and Biology. Immediately afterwards, he put in his candidacy for the World Parliament. Now, he felt a joyful desire for battle, even against dishonest and stupid adversaries.

Harrisson produced his birth certificate; only people of either sex who were between twenty-five and sixty-five years of age were eligible. The provisional lists were very long, but the psychological tests of capability reduced them by a third; about a thousand candidates only exhibited low curves on mental examination, and were immediately eliminated in consequence.

The battle begun with the first strikes was pursued with unaccustomed vigor. Although numerous parties had competed for votes in previous elections, those parties had disappeared, or, rather, had aggregated into two opposed masses. On one side was the parallelist group gathered the majority of manual workers, privileged individuals complaining of oppression; on the other was the meridianist group, which included the most active part of society—the most often guilty of harassment, in fact, but very proud nevertheless and eager to conserve some appearance of superiority.

There was not, among the majority of leaders, any profound or rational conviction. There was, in any case, no real conflict of interest between the two groups, but—which was worse—an absurd sentimental opposition, an increasing aversion born of the long-suppressed appetite for conflict and adventure.

The parallelist party, profoundly influenced by modern philosophy, went into combat with cries of "Liberty!" and "Justice!" Without any valid reason but a rationale of symmetry, the meridianists rallied the enthusiasm of new prophets who opposed to the vague ideas of immature dreamers summary formulae of algebraic rigidity; they extolled authority in all its forms, even the most justly obsolete, and envisaged nothing less than the complete abolition of individual liberty and the installation of a formidably-armed autocratic government—in sum, a sudden and brutal reinforcement of the present organization.

Lahorie had deliberately become the head of the parallelist movement. Harrisson was, by virtue of the force of circumstances, one of the most visible candidates on the meridianist lists. It did not displease him to find himself opposed to Lahorie, against whom he felt a very keen resentment, but he quickly came to feel that he was the prisoner of his troops. He thought that neither order nor justice had ever been a veritable panacea. The truth had to be far from any absolute. Undoubtedly, social life could only be maintained by an uninterrupted succession of reactions of equilibrium, which sometimes ended in one direction and sometimes in the other—but the millennia-old and perpetually-renewed conflict between individualism and a social morality of harsh obligation seemed to him to have already lost much of its importance.

The scientific question was paramount. Above the parties persisting in Byzantine debates, an immense threat might surge forth and suddenly fill the entire horizon. It was necessary to think about avoiding it—and that was the entirety of Harrisson's program.

He had counted on being allowed to develop that program freely and calmly, with the habitual serenity of the scientist. From the very outset, however, he was forced to change his tune.

From the outset, he came into collision with the manipulators of the meridianist party. In their eyes, the organization of scientific work was a secondary issue, which ought to be reserved, because it was incapable of exercising the sentimental leverage on the public necessary to the formation of any great electoral current.

Harrisson resisted, and spoke in all sincerity. Thus, taken to task by a parallelist candidate on the subject of his deposition at the strikers' trial, he declared casually that he thought that he thought the sentence very severe, that he supported the appeal, and that finally, he saw no impossibility in granting the workers a one-hour day.

The following day, the central committee of the meridianists struck Harrisson's name off the list of its candidates, and from all sides, the scientist was accused of seeking success by means of overreaching demagoguery.

Liberated, Harrisson ran his campaign exactly as he wished. As he addressed the crowds and he ran into impassioned and absurd contradictions, the danger became more precise in his eyes. One of the frenetic hours of humankind was doubtless about to chime. He glimpsed formidable possibilities of murder and destruction; he thought about the new elements of an unprecedented subtlety, against which no defense was yet ready.

An immense responsibility weighed upon his shoulders. Lygie sustained his courage. Together, they too sought to translate the truth into simple formulae capable of striking the imagination of the masses.

Untiringly, Harrisson repeated the same warning: the conquest of the ether would be fatal to world civilization if everyone did not cultivate an ever-increasing prudence and a sincere desire for peace. Pressed on all sides by ignorant contradictors, Harrison, with a kind of repugnance and fear, pushed his thinking to the ultimate limit. The scientist, whose passion for research had filled his life, almost came to curse human curiosity. One evening, as he was talking to the parallelists of Asia, he exclaimed: "I tell you that it's necessary before anything else to organize and supervise scientific work. I beg you: either supervise science or kill it. There's no more urgent task. There's no other means of salvation!"

Numerous listeners protested against the novelty of that proposition. Sarcasms did not take long to rain down.

"When are you going to set fire to the Averine Institute?" said the ironic voices. "Smash your apparatus, Monsieur Scientist, and walk on all fours!"

And malign voices also said: "Harrisson! Diabolical Harrisson! You've just admitted that you're one of the greatest guilty men of all time! Demand, then, severe judges who will condemn you to psychic correction! Harrison the Creator, demand from the judges an inoffensive brain of clay!"

Cruelly touched in a sensitive spot, Harrisson left the library, from which he was speaking, and went to the laboratory. Lygie, who had heard everything, came toward him. Leaning on her, he went to the bench on which, in minuscule and complicated apparatus, the mysteries of artificial life were unfolding. There was a steel rod lying on the bench. Harrison picked it up and raised it over the apparatus—but Lygie took action; with all her strength she held the menacing fist in suspension, dragging Harrison to the back of the laboratory.

They were silent for a moment in one another's arms, and the hectic beating of their hearts was audible. Then Lygie spoke. "You mustn't commit such a crime," she said. "You mustn't destroy what might perhaps be, in the near future, the world's good fortune!"

With tears in his eyes, Harrisson replied with devastating certainty: "There's no longer any possibly future. The world has gone mad. Ardent evil might emerge from an inoffensive gesture." For himself alone, he repeated: "Harrisson! Harrisson! Demand severe judges!"

"It's madness," Lygie cried, "to attach such importance to bad jokes!"

"It is, alas, the bad jokes that are right. Yes, all of this, it would be wise to destroy…to destroy our work. Lygie, we require a great and cruel courage!"

Lygie protested vehemently, accumulating arguments. What good would the sacrifice do? Were there not other scientists, countless laboratories? Then again, it was not proven, after all, that people were presently lacking in prudence. Long centuries of peace might yet transpire, which would see unimaginable protective forces develop, thanks to scientists. No, it was necessary not to destroy anything.

Harrisson listened, already half-defeated, glad to be able to yield, but he continued arguing.

"I can't see many reasons for hope. Where are these protective forces? Who will create them for us? The reasons for hope fade away the more attention one devotes to them: a mirage! Humans are mad and wicked, and they can't be otherwise; can one not see that they're dying of *ennui* in the garden of sagacity? Science has developed too rapidly in a world of slow metamorphoses. Averine was born five thousand years too soon, and we, who are continuing the Master's work, insane as we are—insane!—will arm brother against brother, perhaps opening and infinitude of tortures. Perhaps we're opening the door to oblivion!"

Lygie shook her head. "No, no! All that is a nightmare! And what does it matter? It's necessary to know, regardless."

Harrisson raised his head, and, behind Lygie's back, moved gradually toward the apparatus, towards the unknown tempter, toward the fascinating mystery. A quarter of an hour later, heads together, they were leaning over a luminous screen on which the evolution of a microscopic tumultuous organism was being mapped out.

They spent part of the night there, quivering with emotion, their minds closed to external agitations, both repossessed by the most tyrannical love of all.

Harrisson ceased completely to speak in public. His alarm call had, however, awoken a few echoes. About twenty candidates—scientists and philosophers—adopted his program, thus constituting, with no chance of success a weak party on the fringe of the melee.

The battle continued, fervently, between the two great parties of meridianists and parallelists. On polling day, the automatic tellers awarded an indisputable victory to the parallelists; Lahorie was at the head of the list, with a number of imposing voices.

For the first time since the beginning of the Universal Era, a compact, combative and sectarian minority stood up in confrontation with an arrogant majority, attaining power behind adventurous leaders.

Harrisson learned the result without disturbance, and even with a secret relief. At the last moment, he had dreaded the miracle of a success. He was, however, the first to bear the consequences of Lahorie's victory. Before the new elect had even taken their seats, a campaign was launched in the General News against the director of the Averine Institute.

Harrisson took the initiative. He handed in his resignation and, a few days later, in company with Lygie, he left 1.47.

V. Magical Thirteen

Harrison and Lygie took up residence around 0.48,[11] not far from a major generating-station, in a latitudinal alignment of the secondary network.

They moved into a rather isolated house on a hillside, which they had baptized *The Refuge*. The house had been built by a petty artisan and was, in consequence, mediocre in is dimensions, but in a thoroughly modern style and provided with the usual comforts. It received daylight through large bay windows opening between columns of metal and artificial marble. The crystal of the panes let all light through, but a simple mechanism permitted the admirable transparency to be rendered selective, and thus to give the façade, shining in the sunlight, the most delicate tints of the prism. In addition, a series of light insulating shutters guaranteed the house against vagabond radiations emitted by private generators. The energy of the public zones sufficed for heating, lighting and animating the automatic apparatus necessary for everyday life. By means of special relays, a portion of that raw energy could be transformed at will into subtle and varied effluvia, sleep-inducing, tonic, slightly aphrodisiac and slightly exhilarating. Finally, emergency energy was furnished by a radioactive frieze that ran gracefully around the interior metallic lining.

---

[11] If the novel's zero meridian is the Greenwich meridian this location would be between the present locations of Le Mans and Laval, but if it is the Paris meridian 0.48 would be on the slopes of the Loire valley, not far from Orléans. Subsequent topographical descriptions make the latter seem more likely.

Adjacent to the house on one side was a small hangar for an aircraft and a terrestrial vehicle, on the other, a house-builder's workshop. A road with a vitrified causeway descended, between a double row of improved oaks and flowering plane-trees, to the broad and beautiful highway that went around the bottom of the hill, leading to the nearby power-station.

Harrisson and Lygie had transformed the studio into a laboratory, but they only had a banal installation there for experiments of secondary importance. Their true research center was in the basement; they had placed their special generators there, and spent the greater part of their time there, pursuing their endeavors without anyone's help, in the most absolute secrecy.

Harrisson and Lygie lived in almost complete isolation in *The Refuge*. Their only domestic staff consisted of an old couple of subaltern functionaries as devoid of arrogance as the domestics of the Christian era, of whom they were very fond. They had, however, also brought the little mulatto Samuel and the negro girl Flore from the Institute; they were both equally beautiful, but similarly backward, identified in the course of a psychological investigation as curious specimens of neolithic humankind, and welcomed as such into the Averine institute.

On the subject of the two children, there had been long discussion among scientists, because, although they only arrived at knowledge by rough analogies worthy of the brain of a superior anthropoid, they were completely devoid of the aggressive courage and ferocity that was attributed, perhaps gratuitously, to prehistoric humans. They were gentle, idle and cheerful; they were, above all, sensitive to caresses and capable of profound attachment. Flore became sad when separated from Lygie, and any protracted absence of Harrisson's part gave rise to a veritable anxiety on Samuel's part. Thus, it had been necessary, under the threat of seeing the two children perish, to take them to *The Refuge*.

Flore and Samuel even came to play in the subterranean laboratory; unfortunately, that was not without danger.

The two scientists were, in fact, continuing the study of systems of etheric origin, thanks to which they were still obtaining new forms of artificial life. The tumultuous forms, in particular, attracted their attention. Some time before, Lygie had already observed the frequent appearance, in the neighborhood of regradatory vortices, of such forms within protoplasm endowed with ordinary life. In the course of more recent research, she had also seen microbial colonies of very different species undergo strange metamorphoses under the influence of infinitesimal tumultuous nuclei, losing all their singular characteristics and tending toward a median stable type. That hybridization rendered the existence of an individual much longer, severely diminishing in compensation its aptitude for reproduction.

Harrisson's "magical" vortices, which seemed to reverse the chronological order of phenomena— doubtless within very narrow limits not yet accurately defined—also probably had the effect of reversing the course of evolution, taking terrestrial life back toward the state of homogeneity that intelligent minds still considered to be its original state.

Harrisson and Lygie had soon detected a selective action in etheric formations, and careful analytical work had permitted them to isolate a particularly interesting vortical system that evoked tumultuous life even in the human organism. This system, which they designated by the name of "magical system 13," was presently the principal object of their observations. Studying the formation of tumultuous nuclei in tissues with the aid of various biological preparations, they had arrived at the conclusion that these strange parasitic colonies could not maintain themselves, and only had a durable effect in certain elements endowed with an active cellular life. The protoplasm of sexual centers, in particular, constituted the veritable preferred ground of the artificial nuclei corresponding to the principal period of system 13. It produced profound and very rapid changes there: an almost-instantaneous degeneration.

This observation caused Harrisson a certain amount of alarm. Although he was working in complete isolation, entirely apart from public forces, and although the vortices of etheric origin that he produced rarely attained the limit of ocular visibility, he nevertheless thought it necessary to take the most careful precautions. Every item of apparatus was covered by a safety-bell; in addition, Harrisson and Lygie never went into the secret laboratory without the protection of a special insulating garment of their own design.

As for Flore and Samuel, there was no possibility of dressing them in that fashion. It was not always easy, however, to persuade them to leave during dangerous manipulations. Harrisson therefore set up for them, at the back of the laboratory, a kind of redoubt that was closed by a translucent insulating curtain. At a signal from the scientist or Lygie, the two children hastened to that little hiding-place and continued their play behind the closed curtain, without being separated from their masters.

No one else went into the laboratory; even the two aged domestics never went near it.

Harrisson and Lygie kept their work secret, as they kept their new happiness secret. They rarely paid any heed to the General News; the disquieting rumors from outside died on the threshold of their house. Their love illuminated every hour.

Three months passed like that, the best of their life: three months of ardent and tranquil labor, scrupulous and yet exciting research.

Then there was an accident...

Lygie was expecting to become a mother. Fearing some imprudence, Harrison never left her alone in the laboratory. One morning, however, a sudden indisposition kept him in bed—an inconvenience all the more irritating because he was due to observe the results of some important experiments that day. In the evening, Lygie could no longer hold back. Secretly, she went down to the laboratory, but, in her haste, mistakenly put on a smock that had been unused for some time. Then she prepared a microscope and lifted up a safety-bell. A surprise awaited her.

For the initial stimulus, Harrisson had employed two neighboring generators. Within the zone where the two energetic fields had intersected, perhaps for a hundredth of a second, shone a kind of miniature Milky Way. Inside an opaline disk, clearly perceptible by the naked eye, were nebulae, the majority of which had already surpassed the magical period. No such result had ever been obtained before. Lygie arranged the recording apparatus and placed a series of reactive or living colloids within the zone of influence. Then she ran to take the good news to Harrisson.

As soon as she spoke, he uttered a cry; he had just noticed the smock—the useless smock, absolutely transparent to the radiation of magical 13.

Already, Lygie had gone pale, traversed by a sudden pain.

A celebrated American gynecologist, a friend of Harrisson's, was summoned urgently. During the four days that he spent with the invalid, he could only observe singular accidents that plunged him into profound astonishment. Then the morbid symptoms disappeared, and the young woman, who had suffered very little distress, recovered her health. All hope of maternity, however, seemed to have been lost forever.

When Lygie returned to the laboratory for the first time, she had a violent crisis of grief. Harrison, also heartbroken and full of alarm regarding his work, raised his arm again in a destructive gesture...

Once again, however, Lygie stopped the gesture.

To all the reasons for continuing the research, another had now been added, which was absolutely imperious. It was necessary to find the remedy for the harm done.

Harrison remained anxious, however. "We might," he murmured, "land on terrible shores!"

"Only the unknown is terrible," Lygie replied. "Forward! Let's seek the light."

Still tearful, she deliberately lifted up a safety-bell and started up the apparatus to administer the creative stimulus.

Then Harrison drew nearer in his turn. Both of them, with a new ardor and a passionate attention, pored once again over the vertiginous mystery from which a cure for the mutilated wife might perhaps emerge—or unexpected possibilities and, in spite of the threats of the moment, a prodigious blossoming of human happiness.

Sheltered behind the isolating curtain, Flore and Samuel were singing. They took turns to improvise a monotonous chant, which they accompanied by clapping their hands: a strange, slightly sad chant, which seemed very, very distant, as if emerging from the depths of the ages.

PART TWO: THE FRAY

I. The New Order

The consequences of the parallelists' victory initially unfolded slowly. Only three ministers fell in the immediate wake of the elections: the Minister of Public Celebrations, the Minister of Aerial Transport and the Minister of Meteorology.

The five permanent directors of the Supreme Council remained, for the moment, above the fray.

In Parliament, where the parties confronted one another aggressively, there was much talk but little action. The slow technical discussions that had occupied an almost-somnolent assembly for five centuries were succeeded by noisy doctrinal oppositions, a tumult of passionate speeches punctuated by continual interruptions. Sentimental conflicts enfevered the most trivial debate. Political eloquence reappeared, joyful, bitter and ferocious. Young people, previously unknown and often uncultivated, rediscovered, as if miraculously, the oratorical tradition of great popular rabble-rousers, the frantic enthusiasm of the fanatic apostles of the Christian Era, which carried people away. Others, who only had the oral thrust of trouble-makers, nevertheless played their part in the concert, like hounds on the point of being unleashed giving voice at first light, saluting the dawn of a new day with a brutal din

Several weeks went by in stormy discussions without the Parliament undertaking any veritable legislative work.

In the light of those first debates, secondary rivalries had appeared between the representatives of the majority. Personal rivalries emerged first; the great leaders, very ambitious, were overtly jealous of one another. From the earliest days, Lahorie, whose indiscreet lyricism wearied the assembly, had been the butt of the sarcasm of an eloquent and subtle representative from southern Africa, the philosopher Endemios. Although they belonged to the same party, the two men were separated by an increasing hatred.

Eventually, above all, ethnic rivalries became more strongly emphasized by the day. The Asiatics were opposed by the Hindus and Australians. North Americans regarded the more numerous, more active and arrogant South Americans with suspicion. Old fires of hatred threatened to flare up again in Europe between the Nordic and Latin races. An already-noisy hostility existed between the Mediterranean Semites, for whom Lahorie remained the mouthpiece, and the South Africans grouped around Endemios.

Ever since the first meeting of the Supreme Council in the ruins of San Francisco, the seat of power had remained the same. No one, until now, had ever complained about it, for the rapidity of aerial communications rendered the longest voyages easy. Besides which, thanks to improvements of the cinetelephone, the representatives who were averse to personal displacement had been able to take part in debates without leaving home for a long time. In fact, during previous legislatures, there had been numerous legislators, including influential ones, who had never once made direct contact with their colleagues.

Times had changed, though. Endemios was the first to protest against the centuries-old custom that gave one region of the globe the appearance of a capital, without any valid reason. In spite of the resistance of former ministers who had remained in place, the principle of Parliamentary displacement was quickly accepted—but passionate debates were launched regarding its implementation, every country claiming priority over its neighbors.

Historical arguments, once deliberately excluded from all serious discussions, collided violently. There was no region so disinherited that it had not been, in the course of the centuries, the theater of some notable incident, had not seen men destroying one another, and had not served as the lair of a predatory race. The annals of the barbarous ages were gloriously evoked; the honor of having been host to the most prolific slaughterhouses was hotly disputed.

In the end, only eight meeting places were chosen. The first was the 20.30 point in southern Africa,[12] in the heart of Endemios' constituency. In spite of all his efforts, Lahorie could not obtain anything for his own country. Discontent was rife in all the omitted constituencies.

As the reform did not present any immediate danger, the Supreme Council did not put up any resistance—but the reformist zeal of the parallelist majority did not take long to manifest itself in a more disquieting fashion. The party's program included the administrative reorganization of the universal society, the substi-

---

[12] In the west of the present day Cape Province.

tution of the present unity with a federalism whose characteristics remained to be determined. That was the logical end-point of regionalist aspirations that had been incessantly gaining strength for half a century. The unity of the parallelists consolidated again on that question. Immediately, the meridianists formed a bloc; benefiting from the secret sympathy of the executive, they succeeded at first, by means of obstructive legal procedures, in keeping the majority in check. Soon, though, the momentum of the parallelists became irresistible and defied any maneuvering. An adroit direct assault by Endemios swept aside the executive and all the senior functionaries suspected of traditionalism.

From then on, the debates unfurled with a precipitate speed, in an atmosphere of enthusiasm. The doctrinal opposition of the meridianist party was fervently manifest, but did not prevent anything.

The principal of territorial subdivisions was rapidly adopted. Some had, in fact, already existed for some years on the margins of universal legislation, although reluctantly tolerated by the central power. Others were hastily formed, at the hazard of the sympathies and, most of all, the antipathies of the moment, without clearly-delimited frontiers, with enclaves, colonies and complicated entanglements. Vast hinterlands eventually remained, in which the population, pulled in all directions, were still hesitating before joining one formation or another.

The Parliament tried to bring a new order out of that chaos. An initial project of delimitation, which attempted to take account primarily of historical affinities, appeared to be extremely complicated and failed completely. There could no longer be any question of natural frontiers; neither rivers nor mountains, nor the polar icecaps, nor even the immensity of the oceans, separated people in any true sense. Ultimately, it was difficult to create too great a number of subdivisions without dissociating some pre-existing groupings.

The surface of the planet was therefore divided into twelve regions or fatherlands, of approximately equal size and corresponding more or less to the most recent and most distinct ethnic groupings. Their frontiers were marked by the energy zones of the principal network—rectilinear and visible frontiers whose fixity seemed bound to avoid any ulterior argument. There were three regions in America, two each in Europe and Africa, four in Asia and one in Oceania. The seas and the atmosphere were divided into zones of influence in the same fashion.

No one among the elite was yet claiming complete autonomy for these regions. A central power, whose role remained at of coordination, still seemed necessary, and the maintenance of certain essential worldwide services—energy production, the cinetelephone, general transportation—was also necessary. It was even useful to retain a central committee of meteorology and, under certain conditions, an international police.

Within this road frame of universal organization, however, each fatherland could choose its government, regulate production and exchange, education, hygiene, mores and festivals—in sum, to live in a distinctive manner. That implied, of course, the right, and even the duty, to maintain autonomous protective forces: a local police charged with internal surveillance.

While that major upheaval was taking place, the executive led a campaign against the directors whose resistance was anticipated: a cunning campaign of clandestine siege. Endemios, the regent of the General News, managed it with tortuous skill.

The Supreme Council, faithful to its centuries-old politics of temporization, hesitated to commit itself fully. The promulgation of new organic laws that claimed to be instituting federalism finally offered the opportunity for a clear reaction. It opposed a categorical veto to the implementation of those laws. Indignation among the popular masses was fervent. A plebiscite, organized without delay in constitutional form, yielded a crushing majority to the partisans of federalism.

Although beaten, the Supreme Council would not give in. It maintained its position until the fifth plebiscite, opposing nothing but the force of inertia to the imprudent desires of the majority. The situation seemed to be incapable of imminent resolution, and trouble seemed to be brewing.

The deaths of two directors, a week apart, in rather singular circumstances, changed the face of things. The election of the replacements was held in legal form, but cropping up abruptly and unexpectedly, it brought to power an Asian and a white South American, both members of the Academy of Spiritualist Philosophy, second-rank personalities recently brought out from the shadows by Endemios' intrigues.

With them, a new spirit entered into the Supreme Council.

Immediately after the sixth plebiscite, the organic laws were immediately implemented. The directors only maintained their opposition with respect to secondary questions concerning the world police.

Then commenced a period of singular effervescence. It was the confused seething of a genesis.

The builders of the future hastened to assemble their materials, loudly raising their enthusiastic and feverish appeal. Disdainfully rejecting the prudent disciplines of the Universal Era, they worked swiftly and boldly. They did not count among the just or the sage, but the ardor of the summary and sure gesture substituted for the debility of their thought. Like the human leaders of prescientific times they were not precursors but merely fine barbarians, dominated by crudity or mediocre cunning. They had the obstinate courage and trumpeting pride of the great feudal Christians, bold heads of states, armies or gangs. They also had their serene ignorance and profound insouciance.

And behind those blind individuals, the stamping feet of adventurous and credulous crowds could already be heard.

In every fatherland, elections succeeded elections and plebiscites succeeded plebiscites.

The twelve national assemblies met at approximately the same time. The parallelists triumphed almost everywhere. Only two regions, Eastern Europe and Central Asia, gave a majority to the meridianists. Those regions, in spite of the fervor with which the meridianists had fought against federalism, were not the last to organize or to manifest an arrogant mistrust with regard to neighboring countries. Very rapidly, power there was concentrated, in law and in fact, in the hands of a dictator, who was, in Central Asia, a young engineer from General Transportation, and in Eastern Europe, a great industrialist from the Black Lands.

Nowhere else did the assemblies consent to such an abdication. Several regions gave themselves a government modeled, in broad terms, on the universal government. Others adopted a much less stable regime, involving monthly or weekly elections. Central America, finally, instituted a veritable government of the people by the people, without interposed representatives; Parliament

111

was reduced there to a permanence in which a handful of elected functionaries, taking turns from hour to hour, oversaw the publication of political speeches, recorded daily votes and transmitted the popular instructions to the agents of implementation.

In reality, in spite of the diversity of constitutions, the direction of affairs passed everywhere into the hands of a reckless oligarchy. The majority of the representatives in the World Parliament were also part of national assemblies. The influence of the great leaders was preponderant. Lahorie was named consul for life in Northern Africa. Endemios, by contrast, had refused any mandate in his own land, but, as the regent of the General News, disposing of mysterious means of action with regard to the Supreme Council, was one of the masters of the hour. In Southern Africa, his authority was no less omnipotent for remaining occult.

The mental agitation remained extreme. Already, national minorities were describing themselves as oppressed. Strikes broke out, immediately harshly repressed. Vitrification workers sabotaged the road network in Eastern Europe. In Australia agriculturalists destroyed meteorological stations and set traps for the regional crop-inspectors.

The Supreme Council, in which unanimity was now only obtained with difficulty, reacted meekly to the most hazardous innovations; although it still retained the general direction of the world police, it had allowed itself to be gradually stripped of the right to supervise recruitment and the appointment of officers.

The entire society was in the process of renewal; the most cautious ended up giving in to the current and allowing themselves to be carried away.

The moment was dangerous, ardent and beautiful. Humankind, as if by the wave of a magic wand, woke up young. Celebrations surpassed in splendor and animation anything that previous generations had been able to imagine. Every country was witness to a rich artistic flowering. Poets, orators, musicians, dancers and architects created or rediscovered singular forms of beauty. Debauchery diminished; youth devoted itself enthusiastically to physical sports imitative of barbarians. Engineers undertook pointless great endeavors.

And in private laboratories, escaping all control, numerous scientists following in Averine's footsteps searched imprudently in the fabulous matrices of the ether in order to find the secrets that might perhaps make humans as powerful as gods.

National rivalries increased rapidly.

Economic disputes seemed to be in the foreground; they were easily started and magnified at will; they were invented when they did not exist. In spite of everything, their importance remained mediocre, for there were no disinherited countries and poverty was unknown. For a world population almost equal to the population of the Christian apogee, production was much greater. Everywhere, agriculture and industry obtained, with minimal effort, enough to satisfy all essential needs, and also the new needs born at each stage of scientific civilization—but a politics of excessive production began to enfever every government.

The situation seemed particularly tense between Southern Africa and the Lahorist territories, which, extending between the tenth and fourteenth parallels, comprised a part of Europe and the peninsula of Asia Minor as well as northern Africa.

113

In northern Africa, where the intensive exploitation of certain regions had sufficed to nourish the entire population, the Lahorist government nevertheless pushed for the study of great projects, such as the development of immense central expanses that were still semi-desert.

The southern Africans denounced these projects as prejudicial to economic equilibrium, and strove to subvert them. The actions of the Southists, indirect and cunning, often took the form of meteorological sabotage. Clandestine stations, exceedingly mobile, were transported between various points on the equator at the limit of territorial waters, neutralizing the Northern stations and unleashing inexplicable squalls at a distance, dissipating the artificial clouds moved a considerable expense over the desert zone. Accusations also began to be leveled at the Southists of acting by mysterious means on the upper atmosphere, where certain protective layers were destroyed in places, or at least rendered transparent to radiations dangerous to vegetal life.

The Lahorists also excited the jealousy of their neighbors by the considerable development that they planned to give to a national network of aerial routes; they aroused their suspicion by virtue of the feverish zeal with which they brought all the way to the tenth parallel, across the desert zone, numerous causeways with no obvious utility, which seemed designed solely to play a strategic role in an emergency. On these causeways, vitrified by a secret method, sliding vehicles could attain considerable speeds, of the same order as the speed of aircraft.

To these motives for dispute was added a violent religious thrust on the part of the Lahorists. The majority of the religions of the Christian Epoch had almost disappeared at the beginning of the Universal Era, along with other dogmatic systems, but for half a century and in-verse movement of human thought had been observable; the masses were reverting to great consolatory dreams, to antique fables of hope and love. The movement was slow and almost timid, except among the Lahorists, where Islamic islets had resisted all the assaults of ra-tionalism and in which fanaticism was beginning to flare up as in barbaric epochs. From Morocco to Arabia, apos-tles rose up amid the humble; they recovered forgotten grand gestures and the ardent poetry of old legends flowed from their lips. Furthermore, they retained an overly narrow interpretation of texts; broadening the Quranic precepts to the point of symbolism, they adapted the Law to the exigencies of scientific civiliza-tion and loved to proclaim themselves philosophers. They were no less animated by the spirit of adventurous proselytism that had once driven their ancestors to the conquest of the world.

As soon as it was formed, the new government had been obliged, under threat of being toppled, to recognize Islam as the state religion. Lahorie, as consul, had thought it good politics to accept the redoubtable title of Commander of the Faithful. That precaution did not pre-vent his being closely watched and suspected of lack of fervor. The zeal of the religious leaders sometimes caused him serious embarrassment.

That zeal was exercised in a particularly indiscreet fashion with regard to the Southern Africans. Under the pretext that Islamic groups had once existed beyond the tenth parallel, caravans of Lahorist pilgrims periodically penetrated as far as the vicinity of the equator. At the same time, an intense propaganda campaign strove to reach the black populations of the South and bring them back to the Islamic faith.

The Southist government, dominated by Endemios, reacted with all the more violence because serious meridianist agitation was also making them anxious; the international quarrel served to distract opinion from internal political issues.

Endemios had all religious propaganda banned by the General News. Immediately, the Northists decided to install a cinetelephonic network entirely independent of the universal network—but that project ran into the unexpected opposition of the World Parliament, and Lahorie's government dared not proceed with it.

Victorious, Endemios pursued his advantage. It was difficult to forbid access to the territories of the South to Northern travelers completely, so he strove, by roundabout means, to render the great pilgrimages practically impossible.

Islamic fanaticism was increased by that. Because certain parts of the Southern territories were only accessible at the expense of great effort, they acquired the reputation of being holy places. The love of difficulty heated souls; the beauty of sacrifice inflamed them with pride. Numerous pilgrims crossed the frontier in isolation. Their disputes with the infidels or the Southern national police became the object of fine heroic tales; preachers possessed of a barbaric eloquence collected these tales and drew considerable capital from them.

Lahorie and the principal members of the government, called upon every day to take measures against the Southists, saw the time fast approaching when they would no longer be able to contain the religious movement. They were not unduly worried about it, accepting the worst eventualities light-heartedly.

In Southern Africa tranquility was no more prevalent. The meridianist agitation, far from dying down, gained ground. Major agriculturalists, who had emigrated to Eastern Europe, threatened conflict from afar, with skill and tenacity. A *coup-d'état* did not seem impossible. Endemios and his lackeys no longer felt secure. Great gamblers, they had the idea of redirecting the various hatreds abroad, and attempting the supreme wager.

Events unfolded inexorably.

II. The African War

Five *bon viveurs*, South African blacks, representatives in the World Parliament, were returning to their homeland by aerial express along the 330 meridian. Parliament was, in fact, in session in that summer season at point 60.330,[13] not far from the celebrated ruins of an ancient slave capital. The black representatives had not taken a very active part in the debates; nor had they given any more thought of visiting the curious ruins of the ancient capital; but they had taken pleasant excursions over the polar ice-cap, witnessed exciting spectacles and drunk heady wines. They were coming back rather tired but, all in all, content with life. Alone in their cabin, they were laughing, showing sparkling teeth, taking the name of Allah in vain and singing the immodest songs of their homeland.

All went well until the fourteenth parallel, but the express had scarcely arrived over the territory of Asia Minor than Muslim passengers protested. A Lahorist attendant intervened without delay with the singers. She was a daughter of the Aegean islands, a superb young woman with elongated eyes. Forgetting the international law, for which they had nevertheless voted, which obliged them to be respectful, the representatives wel-

---

[13] The previously-conventional system of notion here seems to have been suddenly, and momentarily, multiplied by ten. Using the Greenwich zero meridian, the indicated point would be somewhere in present-day Tanzania, nowhere near any "ancient slave capital," but using the Paris meridian would move it significantly closer to Dar-es-Salaam.

comes the attendant with ardor and joviality. She came out, locked the cabin door and notified the police. At the relay station on parallel 30, the five parliamentary blasphemers were arrested and taken to prison under the insults and blows of an excited crowd. One of them died from his injuries the following night.

In Southern Africa the indignation was intense, and propagated instantaneously. Far from calming the masses, the directive milieux stirred up popular passions. Two days after the arrest of the representatives, an ultimatum was delivered to the Lahorist government—an ultimatum of such intolerable arrogance that the entire world quivered in surprise. The riposte came immediately, in the form of a document of the same kind and an even more acidic tone, in which the Lahorists impudently added to their delirious chauvinism and hatred of their neighbors the aggressive fanaticism of their religious leaders.

Among the world elite there was an instant of alarm. Even those who had no clear idea of the danger experienced a kind of vertigo before that unusual situation. People looked to the Supreme Council, but the directors only gave voice to vague appeals for moderation; dispossessed of their principal prerogatives, and having little confidence in certain elements of the world police, they hesitated over becoming fully involved.

The World Parliament was worried; it had appointed an international committee of arbitration, which made a lot of noise without making any firm decision. In fact, thee ten nations not directly involved retreated discreetly, leaving the field free for the adversaries; they seemed to be waiting, with troubled sentiments in which curiosity held sway over anguish, for the commencement of the fratricidal contest. The situation developed by the hour, in increasing confusion. There was nothing but oblique maneuvers, false news, provocative measures, sly excitements, advances, retreats, lies, belated appeals for arbitration, no-less-belated offers of mediation, countless intrigues of which the most perspicacious observer would have been hard put to discover all the threads. A deceptive mist masked the actions of the great political figures so well that all ulterior research into responsibilities would seem virtually impossible.

No one succeeded in establishing with precision in what circumstances, in what place and by whose fault the hostilities commenced.

Only one point remained indisputable: on the twelfth of June, the fourth day of the celebrations concluding Ramadan, the fighting was general by noon on the zero meridian, and numerous cadavers were already littering the ground all along the tenth parallel. The spectators who were watching the religious celebrations on the frontier by cinetelephone that day were only able to furnish contradictory accounts; according to the point at which they were situated, they put the blame either on the Muslims or on the Southists. The war appeared to ignite spontaneously, everywhere at once.

In *The Refuge*, it was the old domestic Salem who raised the alarm. In his youth, he had served a term as cook in the household of a black horticulturalist whose gardens extended along the banks of the river Comoé,[14] and his son was still out there, an engineer in the fruit section, with the same horticulturalist. Since the storm had been gathering in the region, Salem had been paus-

---

[14] The name of this river is now more commonly spelled Komoé nowadays; it rises in Burkina Faso and flows into the Côte d'Ivoire.

ing anxiously in front of the cinetelephone screen several times a day. At noon on the twelfth of June, having just put himself in communication with the Upper Comoé, the old man recoiled with a cry of fright: the sound of explosions was emerging from the receivers, along with the roar of flames and howls of fury and fear.

Harrisson and Lygie, who were at table in a neighboring room, ran to the apparatus. A sickening scene was presented to their eyes: hundreds of Lahorist fanatics were racing to attack a Southist alignment. In the gardens and around the habitations there was an agitation reminiscent of an anthill. Women were in the front rank, striking heroic poses.

With a trembling finger, old Salem pointed to the middle of the screen at a little house surrounded by the furious mob; already, outbuildings and crops planted around that house were going up in flames. Harrisson narrowed the field of vision; the central image filled the screen—and the door of the house was seen to open abruptly. A man appeared on the threshold.

"Pierre!" Salem cried. "Pierre! My son!"

Harrisson tried to pull the old man away, but he resisted, clinging to the apparatus, his face ravaged by anguish. The scene unfurled before his eyes in its entirety; it was very rapid.

The man attempted to negotiate; a clamor drowned his voice.

"Death to the Southern dog! Put him to the torture! Burn him!"

Women bounded forward, claws extended; projectiles began to rain down. The man seemed to hesitate for a few seconds; his eyes wandered, perhaps in search of help. Suddenly, he raised his arm, and aimed a missile-launcher, at short range. A flame sprang forth, straight at first and then rapidly curving in a spiral—and there was a void in front of the house; a forceful gyration carried aloft, like wisps of straw, tree-branches, stones and human body-parts. The assailants who were on the edge of the danger zone had been knocked down as if by a cyclone.

The shooter himself, obliged to aim at too short a range, was knocked down. He got up almost immediately and started to run, disarmed and haggard, colliding with his enemies. Hands gripped him; he was pummeled and bitten, and disappeared under a cluster of tangled bodies. He reappeared, carried at arm's length as if on a hurdle; his broken limbs hung down. A woman brandishing a torch burned his hands. With loud cries of ferocious joy he was thrown, panting, into a blazing barn.

Salem had fainted. Harrisson carried the old man out and confided him to Lygie. When he returned to the apparatus, he searched the screen in vain for the engineer's house and the Muslim crowd; the aircraft of the two sides had come into play and had already cleared the location.

Harrisson enlarged the field of vision. The entire region was unrecognizable. A few minutes had sufficed for the destruction of an alignment several kilometers long, comprising hundreds of houses. The frightful heat of the disintegrations had ignited an immense conflagration that was devouring all combustible material. Metallic constructions littered the ground, flattened, crushed or even blown apart by the explosions. Trees were lying horizontally, in flames; the earth, holed by huge craters, was covered in blackened and dismembered cadavers. A few fugitives, Muslim or Southist, miraculously saved after that collapse of the sky on their heads, were running at random, breathless in the suffocating atmosphere.

Aircraft were already present in considerable numbers, and more were arriving from all directions: national police machines or civilian craft equipped with independent engines and clandestine weaponry. At first, the pilots had only thought about taking part in the terrestrial riot; some had ravaged the Southist alignment, others had annihilated the Lahorist hordes. Now, that facile task having been accomplished, they were confronting one another in the open sky above the smoke of the conflagration.

The absence of any discipline, the diversity of the machines and the heterogeneity of their armaments rendered the battle confused. It was a matter of singular duels, engagements at hazard, treacherous feints and surprise attacks. A few policemen, equipped with broadradius interrupters, sent older model craft, easily disrupted, tumbling to the ground—but a number of the partisans had improved machines resistant to ordinary influences, with formidable offensive power.

Many aircraft surrounded themselves with opaque clouds, from which they surged forth unexpectedly, hurling thunderbolts from all their portholes. Others rose up toward the zenith, and, when they had chosen their prey, let themselves fall at crazy speed, spitting out a volley of minuscule explosive missiles as they passed, which pulverized the adversary.

After ten minutes of combat, three-quarters of the aircraft had crashed to earth or been blasted apart in midair. None had fled. The same frantic heroism animated all the combatants.

Harrisson, overwhelmed, manipulated the latitude control. Rapidly, his gaze searched the rich territories of the South, and then returned to Lahorist territory, following the meridian alignments. Great agitation was manifest everywhere; numerous aircraft were being hauled out of their garages and taking off; here and there, tumultuous assemblies were forming. Meanwhile, the lands far from the border were still unaffected; no damage or military action could be seen there.

Harrisson had a glimmer of hope; the terrible friction of the advance-guards that he had just witnessed might perhaps have no consequences; arbitration might still intervene...

He returned to the tenth degree of latitude and slid the field of vision along the parallel. Immediately, his hope vanished; that madness of war, this time, truly reigned supreme.

Everywhere from the Atlantic coast to the mountains of Abyssinia, the people of the North found themselves in contact with their Southern brethren, battle was commencing or already raging, or even coming to a climax in a furious orgy.

Cadavers were piling up at the termini of the Lahorist highways. From the very beginning, many of these roads had been cut by Southist aircraft, and the innumerable pilgrims who were arriving via sliders at Bairam festivals had been massacred in a matter of seconds in profound masses before being able to disperse into open country. In some places, thousands of people had been mowed down at a stroke.

The international airports remained intact, but the majority of alignments had been destroyed. There were no victors and vanquished on the ground, merely corpses, howling wounded and a few half-mad runaways.

White, empty patches appeared at intervals on the screen, marking the location of regions where all communication with the rest of the world had been interrupted, and from which all traces of civilization had already disappeared.

Aerial conflicts set the sky on fire. Thousands of aircraft coming from opposed horizons hurled themselves into battle. In the fever of that first impact, no one thought of launching automatic machines against the enemy. All the aircraft were manned, maneuvered directly by courageous pilots. The acrid blood of the ancient barbarians was seething in the arteries of the combatants.

An immense flock of ferocious birds soared over the devastated ground. Aircraft of every shape and size were seen, from fragile dragonfly pleasure-craft to retired General Transport aerobuses, from family vehicles to narrow and sleek racing machines, whose equilibrium was only sure at vertiginous speeds. Authentic combat aircraft piloted by national militiamen were no less numerous and no less active; the partisans dispensed a disorderly heroism.

The frenzy was such that it seemed that none could escape it. At the first collision, the adverse formations melted like wax, and the battle would have come to a rapid end had it not been for the incessant arrival of reinforcements.

Lygie had rejoined Harrisson. At the top of her voice, because of the racket of explosions that was emerging from the receivers, she shouted: "What are the universal police doing? What is the Supreme Council doing? Field hospitals need to be set up…and before anything else, the bandits must be separated! They have to be separated!"

She was trembling, her eyes full of horror, and wringing her hands.

Harrison turned down the volume; the drama seemed to retreat into the distance; nothing could any longer be heard but a dull continuous rumble, like the rumble of a natural storm fleeing toward the horizon. On the screen, however, the frightful spectacle still offered itself to the eyes.

Breathlessly, Lygie repeated: "What is the Supreme Council doing? Aren't they going to send in the universals?"

Harrison made a dispirited gesture. "What can the Supreme Council do now? And what good are the police? The universals are no longer reliable..."

He was still manipulating the controls, seeking communication with the most populous regions of the belligerent countries. The rumor of crowds replaced the noise of explosions. Everywhere, people were preparing for battle. The frontier battle was merely a scuffle of recklessly-engaged partisans, but the great work of destruction was about to begin, for which all the forces of nature, all the heroism of humans and all the resources of their diabolical imagination would be methodically employed.

Clandestine power-stations were summoning their engineers; engines of war were emerging from invisible, presumably subterranean arsenals; heavily-armored mobile meteorological stations were departing for unknown destinations.

Above the valley of the Nile, Harrison framed a cloud of automatic missile-launchers, which, doubtless guided by some Mediterranean power-station, were already flying southwards. He followed them as far as the frontier parallel; suddenly, he saw them disperse like leaves in a storm-wind; they exploded in mid-air in all directions, without having reached enemy territory.

Harrisson started in surprise and leaned forward to examine the screen attentively. Then he called Lygie, who had moved away, her nerves jangling.

"The police!" he exclaimed. "Here come the police, at last! Perhaps there's still hope!"

Flying over the mountains of Abyssinia, a squadron of universals was heading westwards at high speed: a compact squadron preceded by ultra-rapid scouts that were making assessments and clearing the route.

The prestige of the international police remained so great that, in spite of the blind fury of the combatants, a void opened up in front of the scouts. The Africans separated, returning to their bases, or at least keeping their distance, hesitating over what to do. The universals opened up the conflict as the prow of a ship opens up the waves. They advanced straight ahead, sticking to the parallel without maneuvering or fighting. Their active role was limited to interception and destruction, by means of missile-aircraft that were now beginning to fly over the frontier. Some of these aircraft, however, moved by an unknown influence, escaped them and delivered death over long distances.

A second squadron came from the Atlantic. The meeting took place in the vicinity of the 10.40 airport, one of the most important in the general network. From there, patrols were organized and went to line up along the frontier. At the same time, ambulances rose from various points of the globe and headed rapidly toward central Africa.

A few minutes later, Harrisson and Lygie received orders via the General News to report without delay to the laboratory at the 4.48 power-station, where they would receive further instructions.

The Supreme Council, confronted by the immensity of the catastrophe, had pulled itself together and was making a final effort. Conscious of their frightful responsibility, the two new directors shook off the occult yoke of Endemios and, for the first time since their election, the Supreme Council's decisions were made unanimously.

The unleashing of safeguarding actions was carried out with the customary brutality. The directors mobilized the universal police, ordered the complete isolation of the belligerents, the censorship of the General News, the immediate arrest of the African leaders, including Endemios and Lahorie, who were declared guilty in advance of any trial.

From the first moment, however, difficulties emerged. The police responded to the mobilization order without enthusiasm. A number of African universals gave no sign of life; others, as soon as they were armed, had headed for their native countries, not to restore order there but to join the national militias.

The commanders of the legions set an example of indiscipline. They argued their reluctance to intervene against their compatriots and tendered their resignations loudly. Ordered to arrest Endemios, a young engineer, a captain-general in the judiciary legions, refused point-blank to carry out his mission. Defying the law, he neither fled nor hid, but appealed to his troops, to public opinion, and even to the representatives in parliament.

The World Parliament went into permanent session in the 60.330 Palais. Endemios made a speech there. He demanded nothing for himself and declared himself ready to accept any decision of the judges; for his country he demanded nothing but the right to resist an unjustifiable aggression—but he attacked the Supreme Council violently, reproaching it for its blindness and incapacity. He argued that a five-hundred-year-old legislation could no longer be appropriate to modern society. The decision of the directors was not the will of the world; only the Arbitration Commission, in which all the nations were equally represented, had the right to intervene, when circumstances required it.

He did not explicitly demand the resignation of the directors, but others demanded it for him, and the vote was very easily carried.

Abandoned by a part of the police, poorly supported by the rest, the directors could not think of resisting. The Supreme Council was finished.

The Arbitration Committee having recognized that a state of war existed between the two African republics, the representatives of the other ten nations made solemn declarations of neutrality in the name of their respective governments.

The decisions of the Supreme Council were immediately repealed. A few indispensable measures were, however, taken. Large police forces originating in the neutral countries were mobilized; their role was, however, limited to the protection of non-belligerents and the protection of mondial establishments in Africa: the power-stations of the universal network, cinetelephonic stations and those of General Meteorology, and the major arteries of communication.

The *coup-d'état* had taken less than sixty hours. In the meantime, the hostilities, briefly interrupted by the intervention of the universals, flared up again violently.

On the night of the fourteenth and fifteenth, even before the destitution of the directors was known, the flight of missile-aircraft resumed over the continent. The military leaders temporarily abandoned fighting with manned aircraft because it was too slow and ineffective; it was only resumed by a few partisans fond of individual exploits.

The automatic aerial machines traveled incessantly, invisible, silent and rapid. Engineers a thousand leagues away steered them through deserted regions of the sky, easily bringing them back to their flight plan when accidents caused a deviation. With redoubtable precision, they provoked their fall and explosion at the desired point. There was no security anywhere, and the entire population was exposed. Above the scattered habitations of the secondary networks as well as above the overpopulated alignments of the major zones, the clouds suddenly opened and fire from the sky struck the human beings. As if sown by a diabolical hand, the missiles spread out at intervals over the entire extent of the enemy territory, and even over its territorial waters. In a matter of minutes, an entire region was devastated.

It was a methodical, sinister and terribly murderous battle. It reached its greatest intensity on the nineteenth of June, the fifth day. On the morning of the twentieth, the losses were estimated at a tenth of the total population. More than twenty million cadavers littered the earth or were consumed in the flames of conflagrations. The number of wounded was so great, and rescue operations so perilous, that there was no possibility of helping everyone.

More than half of the habitations had been destroyed; those that remained standing were abandoned. People spread out into the country, a long way from the targeted alignments, dispersing as much as they could. People took refuge in caves hollowed out eight hundred years earlier during the Great War of the Christian Era. The majority of these shelters were not deep enough to guarantee real security, but people piled into them even so, for want of anything better. New ones were dug; powerful drills worked relentlessly. By the twenty-fifth of June a substantial part of the population had succeeded in going underground as best it could.

At that moment, the fighting appeared to relent. During the early days, there had been such an enormous consumption of missiles that the reserves of explosive substances had been rapidly depleted. Arsenals had been destroyed, personnel decimated and general production interrupted by the exodus of the population to subterranean refuges.

The hosts of automatic aircraft diminished in number and in size. In addition, the missiles were no longer hitting their intended targets as reliably. New preventive measures were, in fact, being devised. The physicists of the two countries were perfecting new means of defense. By means of special installations, rapidly constructed, attempts were being made to neutralize the energy of the opposing military power-stations. With increasing frequency, projectiles traveling at a height sufficient to escape the influence of manned aircraft, nevertheless deviated from their course. Sometimes, before having crossed the frontier line, they stopped short and exploded as if they had run into an invisible vertical armor; sometimes, too, they were caught in turbulent fields which sent them crashing to the ground, inflicting great damage on the regions where they fell.

The missiles thus became a difficult and dangerous weapon. Manned aircraft therefore reappeared in great numbers, without, however, engaging in all-out conflict. The battle had reached a dead phase.

The Arbitration Committee decided, by a majority vote, to offer its mediation. Via the General News it addressed the people involved in the horrible fratricidal conflict and finally made the voice of reason heard. Among the belligerents, however, the opinion of the masses counted for very little, and could scarcely be expressed. The leaders, absolute masters since the commencement of hostilities, indignantly rejected a premature peace that would have left the adversaries equally diminished and devoid of glory. They consented, however, to a sixty-hour armistice.

A singular and comforting spectacle was then witnessed. From every country in the world, help flowed to the devastated regions. The neutrals came together in a great surge of fraternal pity. The same people who had slyly pushed for war, the same people who had followed all the phases of the catastrophe with an abominable curiosity, hastened toward the battlefields, launching into an astonishing activity, bandaging with an admirable devotion the wounds for which they were, in a way, responsible. The General Services of Hygiene, Medicine and Surgery concentrated all their means of action in a matter of hours. Spontaneously, the autonomous organizations of the neutral countries offered their services and competed in abnegation. Individuals also came running, men and women of all kinds, who modestly put themselves under the orders of the competent authorities, not refusing any kind of work.

The most difficult task was searching for the wounded. Many unfortunates, injured in the first days of the battle, had ended up dying, far from any help, tormented by hunger and thirst. Under smoking debris, moribund individuals were found who had miraculously escaped the flames and asphyxia. Others were found half-buried, yet others moaning beneath piles of cadavers. Gangrene was causing terrible ravages in hideous black wounds crawling with worms. The majority of the wounded were stupefied.

Fast aerial ambulances followed the destroyed alignments. On the broad highways of the general network, sanitary expresses went past at every minute, carrying their lamentable cargoes toward the paradise of neutral hospitals. Nightfall did not interrupt the searches; mobile searchlights streaked the atmosphere and dissipated the darkness around the sanitary or rescue crews. The identification of cadavers was impossible. They were burned on the spot, along with animal cadavers and the scattered body-parts that were found everywhere around the bomb-craters. A formidable stink rose up from various charnel-houses.

At the fifty-ninth hour, the neutrals withdrew, leaving the field free for a second round.

The Lahorists soon obtained a clear advantage. The manned aircraft had recommenced the battle somewhat at hazard, seeking a new method of combat. While the aerial battle monopolized attention in this way, the northern engineers, by means of some of their highways that were still intact, succeeded in mobilizing their Mediterranean power-stations. Transported on appropriate sliders, powerful generators came to reinforce the installations in the frontier zone.

The Southern squadrons were not long delayed in stumbling over this barrage. Many aircraft, suddenly disabled, crashed to the ground. Only the most modern and most powerful aircraft could continue on their route.

The Lahorists, on the contrary, found therein a secure base behind which they could regroup. Their squadrons drove back the enemy and the Southern territories became the only theater of the major actions of the war. The battle became orderly; victory for the Lahorists seemed inevitable. Dominating in terms of the number of aircraft, they imposed their tactics, assuming an incontestable ascendancy over the adversary. Under the protection of rapid scouts who cleared the way, special squadrons sought to hit the power-stations, vital points of enemy resistance. At the price of terrible losses, a few were destroyed and vat regions became easily vulnerable. The Southern population found itself directly exposed to enemy fire. The best caves no longer offered a reliable refuge, for the Northern aircraft blockaded them, obstructing the entrances or bombing them until they collapsed. Half a million unfortunates were this buried alive and died after frightful agony.

The Southists abandoned the caves; furtive groups dispersed once again into the depths of the country, jealous of the combatants in the air, who could at least retaliate. Among the Lahorists, where no one doubted complete and imminent victory, the population, no longer feeling that they were under threat from missiles and enemy aircraft, similarly emerged from the subterranean refuges. In spite of countless bereavements, patriotic and religious enthusiasm was at its peak. To compensate for aircraft that were fighting far away, strategic highways were feverishly repaired. Bands of fanatics piled imprudently on to slides and headed for the frontier. The desire for vengeance was burning in their souls; they wanted to go to enemy territory, to see their suffering and shame at close range. Elementary precautions were neglected; they set out in compact masses without serious weapons, without food-supplies, without even preserving means of retreat in case the highways were cut again.

The Southist defenses were, it is true, weakening by the hour. They still held, however, visibly seeking to gain time, and some of their formations displayed a stubborn energy. They also attempted singular counter-offensives; for that they made use of their meteorological stations. Scarcely efficacious diversions that were limited to brief storms burst out at the same moment at the periphery of enemy territory, at which the Lahorists jeered.

On the fifth of July, signs of lassitude and despair appeared among the Southists.

Cadavers, deprived of graves, infected the atmosphere once again. In numerous cantons, famine was cruelly felt. Lahorist bands had infiltrated south of the tenth parallel, and hideous massacres began.

The Arbitration Committee intervened again; it proposed an immediate cessation of hostilities and the opening of a peace conference.

Drunk with pride, the Lahorists refused; they wanted to exploit their success, demanding that the adversary should surrender voluntarily.

Endemios spoke on behalf of the Southists. His response was clear and simple, worthy of an ancient barbarian chief. "The outcome of the war," he said, "is not settled. There cannot be any question, in any case, of laying down arms while so many dead have not been avenged, and while the vultures of the North are darkening the skies of the fatherland with their sinister wings."

The Southists returned to the conflict with a desperate energy. The rage of the combatants no longer respected international establishments; neutral ambulances imprudently venturing into the battle zone were destroyed. The adversaries found themselves in agreement in demanding the retreat of all the universal services whose safety it had become impossible to guarantee.

Endemios' warning sounded a particularly disquieting note. The Southern rabble-rouser accused the

Lahorists of acts of terrible ferocity; he did not announce reprisals explicitly, but he let it be understood that one might be led to employ, against such barbarians, energetic and unexpected means of defense—and he instructed the universals to withdraw within twelve hours.

This was believed to be a gesture of intimidation aimed at the Lahorists, but Endemios renewed his warning in more urgent terms, and granted a second and final delay at the same time.

The next day, as further bands of Lahorists raced along the Northern highways to reinforce the frontier massacres, the Southerners delivered and unexpected and formidable blow.

They had probably been preparing the surprise in question since the beginning of the war. All their meteorological stations, combining their efforts according to a plan studied in times of peace, took control of atmospheric currents. By virtue of their action, a steady ground-level wind blew from the equatorial forests toward the hot desert regions of the North. On the twelfth of July, the wind suddenly increased; in spite of the dryness of the air, a strange perfume of moldy vegetation became perceptible in the frontier zone. From one ocean to the other, at the same instant, chemical batteries had been automatically unmasked, and were delivering unknown gases to the wind of unprecedented toxicity. An invisible cloud rolled northwards over the entire surface of the continent.

The effects were immediate and terrible; over a mean depth of thirty leagues, death struck implacably. The only ones who escaped were those huddled in the depths of securely-sealed caves, or who were traveling above the poisoned layer. All the sliders that were succeeding one another by the minute along the highways arrived laden with corpses at the frontier stations, crashing into one another.

When the Northern meteorological stations attempted to react it was too late; the sheet had passed and dissipated of its own accord over the deserts, where the gases rapidly lost their toxicity.

The attack was renewed elsewhere in the North in another form. While the Lahorist meteorologists were directing their defensive efforts toward the equatorial region, an invisible scourge threatened more distant lands. For several days, in fact, vast clouds of microscopic crystals had been carried by the rapid currents of the upper atmosphere. On the night of the thirteenth and fourteenth, an immense stormy chaplet suddenly formed above the Mediterranean coasts. The clouds all burst at the same time. Poisoned rain fell in torrents; cisterns and rivers were immediately polluted. When the storm ended, a light asphyxiating mist rose up from the overheated earth.

Again, the victims were innumerable. Millions of Lahorists, their lungs burned and their throats destroyed, were writhing simultaneously in a frightful silent agony. For several hours, a dull moaning, like the immense plaint of the earth, rose up toward the sky, now clear again.

The Southist attack surpassed in horror the greatest crimes of Christian barbarity. The World Parliament, the Arbitration Committee and all the national governments were alarmed. The Arbitration Committee, taking over, by force of circumstance, the role of the Supreme Council, sent the belligerents an order to cease hostilities immediately, in a comminatory tone. The Southist government, moreover, would have to answer for the unspeakable crime committed in violation of human rights and which had also caused the death of neutral agents surprised by the toxic gases in the international establishments of Africa.

The World Parliament voted the mobilization of all the universals.

Events, however, succeeded one another with disconcerting rapidity, The Arbitration Committee's message had scarcely been sent when it learned, with amazement, of the unleashing of a vast microbial offensive. While the Southerners were preparing the gas attack in secret, Lahorist aircraft had, in fact, treacherously inseminated the southern territory. Now, after a brief period of incubation, epidemics broke out everywhere; unknown diseases propagated with disturbing rapidity.

Crime answered crime; the belligerents sank into the same monstrous folly.

The international authorities understood that the time for appeals for moderation had passed; it was necessary to act without delay, and brutally. It was therefore decided to effect the isolation of the two warring nations. The active surveillance of the universals blockaded the frontiers. Great technical councils, charged with tracking events and warding off the unexpected, recalled their specialists. For the second time, Harrisson and Lygie, summoned by the Academy of Physics to the 4.48 laboratory, were obliged to leave *The Refuge*.

A few epidemic nuclei appeared in neutral territory, especially in Europe, Australia and Central Asia; immediately identified, they did not have time to expand. The Hygiene Services remained alert, sand severe measures of isolation were taken in order that the scourge would not overflow the borders of the belligerent countries in future.

It was necessary, in addition, to protect the neutrals from toxic gases. In spite of the recognized expertise of the Southern engineers, their poisoned clouds were causing anxiety; some negligence or error, or even an ever-possible reaction of the Lahorist stations, might cause the clouds to deviate, bearing death to Europeans or Asiatics. The universal meteorological organizations therefore intervened, so energetically that the influence of the African stations was soon nullified.

Unfortunately, the unanimity that had formed among the neutrals at the moment of danger did not take long to disappear. Disputes broke out again in the World Parliament and the Arbitration Committee. From the outset, Endemios had denounced the brutal action of the universal meteorologists as a flagrant violation of neutrality. Annihilating the African stations, he said, was breaking the weapons in the Southerners' hands, while their adversaries—who had been the first blatant transgressors of human rights—retained all their criminal possibilities. The South Americans, the Australians and some Asiatics supported Endemios.

The employment of the universal police also ran into difficulties. Consideration had initially been given to a general action that would have separated the belligerents, imposing an immediate armistice on them, and then peace, but the project soon ran into more or less sincere objections. The non-interventionists held up the danger of epidemics; above all, they affected to dread unexpected resistance on the part of the Africans, a considerable enlargement of the zone of operations, and perhaps a worldwide catastrophe. Their opinion prevailed.

On condition that the belligerents would renounce gaseous or microbial poisons, it was decided to maintain neutrality, while waiting for an opportunity to present itself to intervene without risk.

The police received orders simply to reinforce the surveillance services. The universal meteorological stations, whose sudden and massive intervention had not failed to produce grave perturbations in the neutral countries, reverted to moderate and divergent actions that left a certain autonomy to the belligerent stations, while assuring a relative security to bordering countries.

In the great technical councils, there were discussions regarding the world network, from which the combatants were drawing energy freely. Some engineers had advocated the pure and simple destruction of the African sector, a heroic remedy that would doubtless have considerably diminished the offensive strength of the belligerents but which, on the other hand, would have rendered the ulterior organization of aid and resupply very difficult. Besides which, that was an enterprise without precedent and the physicists dared not affirm that it would not have catastrophic repercussions on the entire network. They hesitated to take the immediate risk of a worldwide upheaval. The majority of the scientists proposed a less radical and less hazardous solution. It was only necessary, they said, by some means yet to be discovered, to render the energy of the public network unusable by the engines of war presently employed.

That was Lygie's opinion. Harrisson, on the contrary, fearing that an unknown evil might afflict humankind entire, had advised destruction. Confronted by the resistance of his colleagues, however, he had to give in. And either at *The Refuge*, with Lygie, or in the 4.48 laboratory, whose direction he had taken over, he searched day and night for a means of forbidding the belligerents the practically inexhaustible energetic reserves of the world network—but the difficult problem remained unresolved.

In that period of universal anxiety, the scientists, momentarily eclipsed by the great politicians, recovered their place in the foreground. The masses instinctively looked in their direction; the essential safeguards were expected as a result of their efforts. And among them all, Harrisson—Harrisson the Creator, Harrisson the successor of Averine—seemed most capable of finding the elegant and audacious solution that would extract humankind from the impasse into which it had foolishly ventured. The superiority of Harrisson was, at any rate, recognized by the elite, and the most celebrated scientists solicited the honor of aiding him in his research.

While this work was going on in the neutral laboratories, the African scientists did not remain inactive either. Relentlessly, they armed the moribund but still determined peoples.

After the gaseous and microbial poisonings, the struggle relented somewhat. The African Sanitary Services having been disrupted, the epidemics had spread very rapidly from the South to the North, and the population had been decimated once again. One the first moment of stupor had passed, though, the survivors had returned to the battle.

The outcome of the conflict once again appeared quite uncertain; death had equalized the chances. The most tenacious would be victorious—or the most ferocious, or the cleverest. Perhaps, in fact, there would only be vanquished.

The ardor of the early days had given way to a somber and patient heroism. The leaders no longer intoned songs of bravery, but their unbreakable firmness was expressed in economical, dry and harsh formulae.

Among the masses, an immense lugubrious pride was dominant: the pride of pushing back the limits of the possible, of suffering as no people had ever suffered before in the scientific era. Hatred vanished; no one any longer dared focus on anything but the objectives of the war. The struggle continued, perhaps less to destroy the adversary as to write a fabulous passage in the annals of humankind.

The microbial war had been abandoned and the vast meteorological offensives had become impossible. On both sides, however, in spite of the undertakings given, they still had recourse to toxic gases. All familiar weapons were employed concurrently. The battle, less intense than in the early days, took on more various aspects but remained no less murderous. The belligerents made broad use of the energy of the general network. New kinds of missiles appeared every day. Manned aircraft no longer grouped together in dense formations, but a dust of squadrons took to the air—and all of them bombarded, blasted, inflamed or poisoned.

Isolated craft risked landing in enemy territory when a good opportunity for massacre offered itself. Women often succeeded in that horrible exploit; disguised as nurses, they mingled with the crowds, and penetrated by trickery into ill-guarded caves where they sowed minuscule engines of explosive disintegration.

Endeavors were decisively interrupted; nothing was any longer arriving from neutral countries; food-supplies were rapidly running out. A frightful mortality afflicted the weak, children and old people. By the fifteenth of August, half the population had disappeared; the number of victims reached two hundred million.

On that date, Harrisson announced to the Academy of Physics that he had reached the goal; it was henceforth possible, without great risk, to neutralize completely, for a long period, the African sector of the general network.

In order to do that, however, it was necessary to obtain the active collaboration of the different national services. The meridianist dictators of Eastern Europe and Asia then demanded further experiments and supplementary guarantees. Their evident ill will caused precious time to be lost, of which the belligerents took diabolical advantage.

It was, in fact, at that moment that the war veritably took on the form of an entirely modern scientific enterprise, and scourges of an astonishing strangeness descended upon human beings.

The recent discoveries of the etheric physicists were utilized.

The African rivals of Harrisson, Takase and the great specialists, brought into play unknown and prodigiously subtle elements. They risked insensate actions with unforeseeable consequences, from which they did not even seek to protect their compatriots. In laboratories in constant communication with the zones, they multiplied creative stimuli gauchely, and vast magical systems were born at hazard in the energetic field of the general network. Fortunately, no other physicist having gone as far as Harrisson in the study of etheric forces, it was only a matter, as yet, of abortive systems rich in antagonistic elements, and, in consequence, largely ineffective.

Perhaps once in every hundred attempts, however, a particularly active system was produced, and that sufficed for people to fall prey to disconcerting tortures.

On the fifteenth of August, a young Southern physicist achieved, after many fruitless attempts, a first success. Thanks to him, at the first light of day, a long magical cloud was produced over Egypt, following the meridian zone 330. The system evolved fully in ten minutes. After a period of intense luminosity, the cloud was extinguished and disappeared in the light of the rising sun. No one, at first, saw any cause for alarm. A few hours later, however, the death of a great many animals was observed; all vertebrates, with the exception of mammals, were exterminated. As for vegetables, as the sun rose, they let their leaves droop—shriveled and blackened leaves that one might have thought afflicted by fire. Among humans there were several sudden deaths and a few cases of blindness, but generally, the damage was slight; it was usually limited to painful dermatitis.

That was only a warning.

On the evening of the same day, following the 20 meridian, four active magicals appeared simultaneously, born of the same stimulus, but different in the mode of their evolution and their effects. The next day, hundreds of them formed.

Like parasites, they populated all the principal energy lines and almost always developed in the lower atmosphere. A few remained invisible but many others were manifest by virtue of very variable luminous phenomena. Violet or blue nebulae were often seen to appear, similar in appearance to the colored artificial clouds with which meteorologists had long known how to populate the sky for the pleasure of nocturnal celebrations. There were also rings of greenish mist rising from the ground like innumerable fire-follets, and silver haloes, a bright radiation around a dark central nucleus, and even long floating comets. More rarely, an immense luminous serpent would coil itself around the imaginary axis of a zone of energy, or a fireball would roll capriciously, jolting over the pathways in the sky and disappearing in a dazzling apotheosis.

Almost always, the phenomena provoked enormous variations in temperature and the disruption of machines employing artificial disintegration. Almost always, too, atmospheric ozone was destroyed, and living beings were exposed, without a protective screen, to redoubtable solar radiations.

The radiation produced by certain magicals was, however, even more dangerous. That radiation often caused rightful dermatitis in humans. The skin, even when protected by thick clothing, instantly reddened and came out in enormous blisters; death followed after a few hours of atrocious suffering. A number of unfortunates perished in this way, flayed alive. Those who were only afflicted by muted radiations survived, but retained an astonishing sensitivity; the merest light was unbearable to them, and they had to live in almost complete darkness.

On other occasions, it was the internal mucous membranes that were damaged, or even the most resistant sheaths of the vascular system.

Often, finally, in the deep glandular masses, certain elements would begin to proliferate at an unprecedented speed. The pancreas or the spleen, the salivary or sexual glands, the kidneys or the thyroid body, attained a extraordinary volume within a matter of minutes, and caused the other organs to wither. Sudden excrescences formed on different parts of the body. Monstrous neoplasms grew like mushrooms.

It was often impossible to determine the precise moment when the individual died, for the most extraordinary forms of artificial life, retarded or tumultuous, continued to animate the corpses, sometimes for hours.

And there was, in certain charnel-houses, a hallucinatory gesticulation of larvae. Heads were detached, torsos seesawed; deformed limbs, enlarged into clubs or ramified like branches, slowly reared up. Ribbons of plastic substance emerged from the cadavers and slithered like insidious reptiles; strange filaments assembled into multicolored tresses. Frightful gleams wandered; tremulous green stars lit up in the depths of vitreous eyes.

In addition, the cadavers decomposed with unusual rapidity. In a few minutes, the flesh was completely liquefied, and when night fell, every skeleton seemed to be floating in pallid water, surrounded by a large halo.

The surviving population was, once again, stunned by amazement. The leaders of both sides seemed disorientated. Firearms and toxic gases were no longer employed. Physicists alone continued the battle. Some of them began to acquire a certain virtuosity in the manipulation of the new elements, From the twentieth of August on, the number of magical creations increased considerably. Their effects continue to defy all anticipation.

On the twenty-second of August, in Southern Africa, a large number of modestly-sized systems were seen to evolve which seemed to have no effect, but the following day, nervous and psychological troubles of an infinite variety and extreme gravity were observed in people exposed to the radiations: partial or total paralysis; sensory aberrations; hallucinations; various phobias; crises of hilarity or terror; ambulatory or lubricious mania; and furious delirium.

In the meantime, the highly-placed neutral politicians, in spite of the urgent advice of Harrisson and the scientific Academies, continued arguing.

Finally, on the twenty-third, triumphing over all the isolation measures, a magical series propagated around the globe, following the twin equatorial zones. Significant etheric systems were born at all the meridian intersections, and formations also appeared at other parts of the general network on either side of the equator. For the first time, the creative stimulus had resonated indefinitely, awakening distant echoes in the immensity of the telluric ether.

In America and the islands of the Malay Archipelago, fifty thousand people were afflicted by extravagant cancers and died within the same minute. In southern Asia, secondary systems, perfectly invisible and probably subterranean, provoked the appearance of a terrible malady among the population of the Hindu alignments, reminiscent of the most dramatic forms of rabies.

It required nothing less than that catastrophe striking the neutrals for the scales to fall from the politicians' eyes and to put an end to all hesitation. On the twenty-fifth of August, at noon on the zero meridian, following Harrison's instructions, the energy of the Africa sector was finally rendered unusable. At the same time, considerable forces of aerial police crossed the frontiers of the belligerent countries from all directions.

Practically disarmed, the Africans offered no serious resistance to the advance of the universals. The neutral police occupied all the international establishments, power-stations, meteorological stations and laboratories, and took control of the means of communication.

The international war was over.

More than two hundred million Africans had been killed. The survivors, having reached the limit of human resistance, fell into a bleak depression.

Aid flowed in; immediately after the police came the ambulances and food convoys.

Soon, the arrival of the emigrants was also seen: major agriculturalists, chiefs of industry and distributors: all the meridianists who had fled the tyranny of Lahorie or Endemios. Before the wounds had even been dressed, they came to reclaim their property, resentfully. Overtly supported by the meridianist governments of Eastern Europe and Asia, they also came to reanimate the ardor of their partisans and demand that the parallelist riff-raff be held accountable for the misfortunes of the fatherland.

For a few days, Harrisson's renown eclipsed that of the noisiest politicians. The General News called him the savior of humankind. In the 4.48 laboratory, where he was still resident, he could not always escape the curiosity of the crowds, and the cinetelephone reproduced his words and gestures far more often than he would have desired. Skillful in following the flux and reflux of popular sentiment, the same journalists who had once attacked him stupidly were now singing his praises. Scientists also rendered him full justice; there was no one, including the famous and conceited Roume, who did not salute him as the world's premier physicist. The director of the Averine Institute offered to resign in his favor. Harrisson refused. His immediate task of preservation concluded, he wanted to step back into the shadows.

On the first of September, aboard a modest private aircraft, he left the 4.48 alone, almost furtively. As soon as he arrived at *The Refuge* he broke off all communication with the General News and categorically refused to receive visitors.

After days of labor and anguish, he experienced an immense lassitude and a profound sadness. The danger, so loudly and so vainly denounced, had now appeared to all eyes—and even though the insane heroism and imprudent ferocity of humans was momentarily appeased, it was still prowling on the imminent horizon.

Harrisson allowed himself to be taken to the underground laboratory, where Lygie had some remarkable results to show him. He darted a long rancorous and loving glance at the delicate apparatus that he had once tried to annihilate, in a moment of desperate clairvoyance.

Now, it hardly mattered whether these redoubtable marvels had been destroyed or not; other physicists had launched themselves boldly along the secret path. They were about to catch up with Harrisson, perhaps even to surpass him.

In truth, there no longer remained much chance of salvation. The danger was so complex, could take such various and unexpected forms, and attain such crazy proportions, that it would be very difficult always to remedy its harmful aspects. The offensive weapon definitely had the advantage over the shield.

Harrisson, his shoulders slumped as he thought about a possible resumption of hostilities, murmured: "It will be the end of everything!"

But Lygie was talking. She was not in despair—quite the contrary. Why should they not succeed in neutralizing the influence of harmful magicals? Since she had been working on her own, she had continued the study of system 13, which she was now able to produce with extraordinary facility. She thought she had discovered that the radiation of the system had effects much less simple than had originally been supposed. By carrying the analysis further, it would doubtless by possible to eliminate all harmful action. Soon, it would undoubtedly be possible to create beneficent tumultuous colonies that would rejuvenate the tissues, cure the sick and the infirm and might perhaps permit the modeling of the humankind of the future, perfectly healthy and beautiful.

Harrisson was not convinced. He kept silent, though, for Lygie was talking in a voice tremulous with emotion, and he divined the words she was not speaking: the tenacious hope of the injured spouse, the egotistical and passionate expectation of some miraculous cure.

The next day, however, an audacious reporter from the General News, passing himself off as an inspector of Domestic Staff, forced his way into *The Refuge*, and Harrisson allowed his secret thoughts to be extracted.

"Humankind," he said, "can no longer be saved by anything but a return to prescientific barbarity."

The reporter, who wanted nothing so much as a sensational declaration of paradoxical quality, went away rubbing his hands, delighted with the success of his cunning.

III. The Meridians versus the Parallels

The ravages of the war confounded the imagination. They effaced the lamentable memories of the Christian twilight.

No African alignment remained intact. Almost all the houses had been destroyed; also destroyed or gravely damaged were the terrestrial communications, the national power-stations, the principal agricultural and market-gardening endeavors, and the distribution facilities of every sort.

Among the surviving population there were few completely healthy individuals. Those who, by some miracle, had escaped the firearms, the epidemics and the magical radiation were exhausted by anguish, fatigue and hunger. If the catastrophe had not quite reduced the entire society to savagery, it had, at least, shaken it severely.

The immense African bloodstain was an ugly wound in humanity's side. It did not take long to provoke confused reactions: a permanent fever whose malignity could only increase.

At first, help came from all sides. No difficulty or danger deterred the ardent zeal of the initial saviors. Ten days after the cessation of hostilities, the African population was safe from famine almost everywhere, and the universal sanitary services were already countering the epidemics.

That was only one part of the task, however—the most urgent, doubtless, but also the easiest. The restoration of the devastated countries was a much more complicated enterprise.

A world commission of specialist engineers had, at the very outset, drawn up a general plan, excellent from the technical viewpoint—but national and political rivalries rendered the execution of the plan impractical.

At the same time, in fact, as charitable individuals hastened to help the victims, without any egotistical hidden agenda, national governments and party leaders were thinking about profiting from the new situation. The vast territory of Africa, where the whole social edifice had just collapsed, a territory once so rich, which could not fail to recover its prosperity after a brief interval, was a very tempting prey on offer to megalomaniacs.

To be sure, no nation had the slightest material interest in establishing its authority beyond its frontiers; such an enterprise would, on the contrary, involve serious difficulties and great risks. Great barbaric dreams of domination, perhaps useful for millennia, still explicable in early Christian times, when every group of humans had difficulty ensuring its subsistence, were nothing but a dangerous and flagrant absurdity in the modern epoch—but they also seemed a gorgeous imprudence, an ardent principle of life, a political rejuvenation of races; and by virtue of their very absurdity, they warmed the hearts of the new peoples: hearts that were still primitive, always stormy and astonishingly backward.

The two meridianist governments of Europe and Asia, which had taken in the numerous African emigrants, found themselves in a privileged situation. They favored the return of the emigrants overtly, and supported them in the most audacious claims for compensation. At the same time, they encouraged an intense meridianist propaganda in all the countries of the world.

The parallelist party, in fact, having been directly responsible for the African war, did not emerge from the adventure well. Everywhere that it held power, aggrieved minorities were emboldened, looking for leadership to Eastern Europe and Central Asia, the double citadel from which the meridianist spirit was beginning to extend over the world again.

In Africa, when the universals arrived on the twenty-fifth of August, all appearance of government had vanished. The organization of the initial aid had been obliged to operate somewhat at hazard, outside any local authority, none being there to offer its collaboration. Soon, however, the imperious voice of the émigrés was heard. Although most of them were naturalized Europeans or Asiatics, they claimed to speak on behalf of their African compatriots, and substituted themselves for the almost-extinct parallelist authorities.

In Southern Africa, their success was easy and immediate. After a simulacrum of popular consultation, a triumphant provisional government assumed power and charged a legislative commission composed exclusively of former émigrés to lay the foundations of a new constitution. Exhausted and inert in the midst of the ruins, the population remained indifferent to this change of masters.

In Northern Africa, the enterprise was slightly more difficult. From the outset, it was complicated by the religious question. Muslim islets formed, which received foreign aid grudgingly, and cut themselves off as much as possible from the rest of the world. On the other hand, the immediate neighborhood of the parallelist republic of Western Europe hindered the meridianist machinations. Spain and Southern Italy were detached from the African continent; the émigrés only had veritable control over the southern part of the Lahorist territories. The nation of Northern Africa was in pieces.

The Southern émigrés, however, secured their domination. Scarcely had it formed when the new government gave its politics a disquieting orientation. The triumvirate maintained a constant liaison with the foreign meridianist dictators, from whom they received directions and subsidies. The legislative commission had laid the foundations for a constitution modeled on the constitution of Eastern Europe, which would permit an extremely centralized meridianist authority to impose itself harshly on the parallelist masses. Finally, the Southist leaders did not hide their intention of lending a hand to the Northern émigrés in order, they said, to remedy the anarchy into which Lahorist society had descended.

All that still remained somewhat theoretical—but meridianist tyranny was, nevertheless, threatening the African continent, and even the entire world, by the projected constitution of a solid and continuous bloc whose geographical center would be Eastern Europe.

The parallelist governments were alarmed and, without delay, demonstrated by their actions that they intended to resist the maneuver. Endemios had taken refuge in South America; the triumvirate, which had immediately laid charges against him, demanded his extradition. The Americans refused point-blank; they declared that any actions taken by the meridianists against Endemios would expose its authors to immediate and severe sanctions. The Western Europeans became guarantors, under the same conditions, of the security of Lahore and his associates whom they had taken in. In addition, when meridianist propagandists attempted indiscreet maneuvers in Spain and Italy, they had them arrested without warning.

From that moment on, one incident was followed by another. National rivalries were not the only, or even the most important, causes of trouble; the political quarrels agitating each country took the complication of a situation that was already very confused to the extreme.

The work of African restoration was definitively compromised. The great agriculturalists and engineers charge with the distribution of aid were engaged in a daily struggle against the agents of transportation, whether or not they were their compatriots. Conflicts of authority multiplied; continual friction paralyzed all the efforts.

An immense international program of temporary constructions, which ought to have furnished shelter for the homeless within a matter of weeks, failed miserably without even having built the indispensable hospitals, food stores and public establishments necessary for the intensive utilization of the general network.

Immediately, private societies entered into play. They were, in reality, national enterprises subsidized more or less frankly by the various governments. Each country pushed its own, seeking to carve out a zone of influence and to create, in one form or another, an African colony. The two meridianist governments, which were closely linked to the triumvirate, quickly took action to drive out their rivals. The South Americans, the Australians and the Western Europeans then appealed to the Arbitration Committee. Unfortunately, they did not wait for its decision; as soon as their claim was formulated, they took direct action. Their propagandists succeeded in provoking a rebellion of the subaltern workers on the temporary construction against the engineers, so effectively that the materials that had been sent to get the work under way still remained unused.

The quarrel also had a violent repercussion in the two meridianist nations. Politically-motivated strikes broke out, and the movement gradually attained a considerable breadth. One by one, the transport workers, meteorological workers, domestic staff, the low-ranking personnel in the power stations and the vitrifiers joined the construction workers. In Eastern Europe and Central Asia, there was a mobilization of all the aggressive elements of the parallelist minority.

In spite of encouragements from abroad, the strikes failed. Reacting energetically, via their militias, composed of reliable men, and the great agricultural and distribution organizations, which threatened to starve out the parallelists, the governments disaggregated the enemy bloc and smashed the movement.

The domestic personnel and power-station workers were the first to give in; then it was the turn of the meteorologists and construction workers. The adventure cost them the few liberties they had left.

The vitrifiers and transport workers held out for longer. They only capitulated after numerous acts of sabotage and angry skirmishes in which the militias made use of their weapons.

The governments abused their victory. In the wake of summary judgments, cruel punishments were inflicted on the vanquished who demonstrated particular stubbornness. A hundred vitrification and transport workers were executed, more than a thousand sentenced to psychic correction. For the rest, the situation soon became untenable. Rather than submit to daily harassment, many preferred to move abroad. Twenty thousand people thus transported their hated of meridianist dictatorship to other nations. Thanks to these emigrants, political agitation, already acute throughout the world, gained further intensity.

Any concerted international action having become impossible by virtue of that fact, the plans for African reconstruction were completely abandoned. The renewal of essential food supplies continued, thanks to private initiatives, but interminable lines of rubble still marked the location of the destroyed habitations. The factories seemed to be permanently dead, and a dismal wild vegetation invaded the marvelous gardens of the equatorial zone, formerly the most beautiful in the world.

Africa, however, still served as a dueling-ground; there, in fact, the two great parties that divided the planet collided more acrimoniously than anywhere else. From day to day, the national rivalries lost their significance; each government spoke, not in the name of an entire people, but in the name of the party in power. Thus, in spite of the entanglement of interests and passions, the formation of two clearly opposable camps became evident, whose contours were modified by incessant political fluctuations: on the one hand, the parallelist powers, of whom the South Americans and the Australians were the most enterprising champions; and on the other, the meridianist bloc, seemingly smaller in size but more compact, and supported in the opposing camp by growing minorities.

For each group, the restoration of the devastated regions was no longer anything but a pretext for attempts at domination.

Riots broke out, particularly frequent in Africa. Mysterious accidents occurred whose causes were not passionately investigated by the responsible governments.

In the meantime, the tone of diplomatic conversations remained, if not courteous, and least formally polite. It was merely a question of justice, arbitration and human rights! A prudent hypocrisy masked the brutality of intention. The cataclysm that had just bloodied the human race was too recent, its effects still too visible, for anyone to dare to talk about war. No one knowingly wanted war. No government would have dreamed of taking on the frightful responsibility. Political struggle, said the great leaders, doctrinal opposition, not hatred for peoples. And they said it again, as in the course of a simple election campaign; it was not a matter of fighting but of counting.

Unfortunately, riots, conspiracies, criminal actions and uprisings were on the increase, and not merely on African soil, where the most agitated elements of all races were seething like variegated foam, but everywhere, even in the calmest regions, where governmental authority remained solidly grounded. In every country, the minority, harassed by the party in power and provoked by foreign propaganda, attempted violent redress, seeking by every possible means to expel the masters of the moment.

The meridianist doctrine was still gaining ground. In Southern Asia, the two parties had arrived at parity. In South America and Australia, the great agriculturalists formed a powerful and active minority; the parallelist government had difficulty warding off its opposition, and seemed vulnerable to an audacious coup.

In Central America, where the referendum system was still functioning, popular votes followed one another in quick succession by the hour, bringing the permanent executive committee absurd and contradictory instructions. After a fortnight of complete anarchy, a handful of meridianist agitators seized power. Popular consultation was suppressed and the dictatorship of a meridianist oligarchy began to weigh upon the land. The functionaries of the permanent commission, enlightened individuals long accustomed to the quotidian fluctuations of politics, allowed themselves to be dismissed without resistance, but a section of the police force resisted; a few principal engineers in command of legions, who had sworn fidelity to the parallelist constitution, stood up energetically against the usurpers. They soon succeeded in rallying their troops, and also specialists in the transportation and cinetelephone industries. The mass of the population remained undecided; it followed, without taking any active part therein, the struggle between the rival factions, formed of elements that were still not very numerous, but audacious and determined to emerge victorious.

There were bloody disputes from the outset. Two parties of militia encountered one another by chance, with no other weapons than police truncheons, but confronted one another nevertheless in pitched battle, like the barbarian warriors of the remotest ages. That affair, both dramatic and farcical, was followed by numerous far more serious encounters, in which the militiamen's weapons caused ravages, not merely among the combatants but also among the peaceful population.

Each partly openly received help from abroad. Refugees who fled to neighboring countries came back therefrom comforted, armed and supported. The troubling faces of adventurers appeared from all directions. The existing forces grew rapidly by virtue of these continual reinforcements. Their violent action aggravated the fever consecutive to the African adventure throughout the world. In every nation, the somersaults of political life became more rapid and harder. The World Parliament and the Arbitration Committee, where the two great currents of opinion collided as they did everywhere else, were paralyzed.

Everyone still refused, however, to envisage the eventuality of a veritable war. No clear vision of the danger imposed itself on the crowds; it even escaped many intelligent minds. National chauvinism, the direct cause of the recent catastrophe, was marked by political passion; the present discord was not seen as anything more than a slightly heated dispute of parties. War was execrated, and in the General News, pacifist preachers alternated curiously with the inflamed speeches of the most imprudent polemicists.

The situation got worse by the hour. What little survived of international organizations disappeared or was reduced to utter impotence. The universal police, harassed by the propaganda of the two parties, was more an element of disorder. The slightest incident could have enormous repercussions.

Although no large-scale military action had yet taken place, the battle was overflowing the national frame everywhere. Diplomatic protests multiplied in the midst of general inattention. The game was no longer being played by rival nations but between champions of two camps that embraced the entire world population. Asiatics and Europeans were mixed up in American discords; Americans and Australians led the fight against the meridianist dictators of the old continent.

Endemios, who was in hiding among the Brazilian parallelist population, was abducted by yellow aviators in the service of the African triumvirate; rescued by Australians and recaptured by Asian meridianist partisans, he disappeared in a battle between universal police over the China Sea.

Threatened by the same fate, in spite of the protection of the parallelist government of Western Europe, Lahorie spread a rumor of his death and, in disguise, went to ground with his mistress, the dancer Sylvia, in a parallelist French alignment not far from *The Refuge*.

Party leaders could not find complete security anywhere, for frontier violations were no longer countable. Although all relations had been broken off between Central Asia and South America, the yellow minorities, who had resumed the struggle against the meridianist dictatorship of their homeland, were receiving support from their American political coreligionists; in retaliation, the Asiatic agriculturalists lent a hand to the growers of the pampas. The situation, apparently still extremely confused, was nevertheless moving in the direction of simplification. The singularities of the two camps were becoming increasingly distinct.

A strike of vegetable-growers, who were soon joined by almost all the engineers and agriculturalists in the whole world, took the conflict into a new phase. Provoking swift reactions of immense breadth, it marked the beginning of a series of irreparable misfortunes.

The frenetic moment was approaching in which all civilization was to collapse, and when the question would be raised of the very existence of the large, cunning and powerful primate, dominant for millennia by virtue of its heavy and disturbed brain, in which the dream of life was organized in indefinitely perfectible theories. There was a gradual imperceptible slide from violent political agitation to a veritable state of war.

In the beginning, each party claimed to be acting solely by means of energetic pressure, perhaps contrary to human rights but nevertheless excluding recourse to offensive weapons. It was a time of great strikes; strikes by vegetable-growers, grain-producers, livestock-breeders and distributors, with immediate ripostes from transport workers, meteorologists, cinetelephonists and power-station workers. The meridianists threatened to starve society, the parallelists to paralyze it. There was no lack of tragic incidents in consequence. In several regions, producers were expropriated by force; elsewhere they resisted victoriously. Distributors were hanged and clandestine reserves pillaged. Power-station workers attacked meridianist building-workers and destroyed their installations.

Gradually, all the groups that attempted to maintain neutrality were led, however reluctantly, to take sides. After three weeks, the conflict was general; society was on the brink of the abyss.

And yet, there were still people to be found to argue that these were slightly serious teething troubles, an ordeal from which humankind would emerge purified, provided with a new and salutary discipline!

People refused to admit the state of war.

The situation was, it is true, unprecedented. Neither the mediocre national adventures of the prescientific era, nor ancient religious and civil discords, nor the Great World War of the Christian twilight, nor even the recent African war, could compare to that total effervescence: a strange duel in which the two parties were in contact everywhere, and it was impossible for them to hold any ground.

The first phase of the conflict was chaotic; there was no overall plan, no discipline, no logical coherence in the conduct of operations. Leaders surged forth suddenly one day, but, immediately toppled, plunged back into obscurity. Crazed groups spread terror with blind fury. Abrupt panics and barbaric charges were seen, hideous treasons and sublime devotions, a formidable gasp of the masses, dragged by seemingly-fateful forces toward inconceivable adventures.

Events were inextricably entangled in space and time. They defied all anticipation. When large-scale endeavors failed, it was not rare to see slight shocks resonating strangely, violence propagating in undulations of increasing amplitude.

During this period, whose duration did not exceed a fortnight, all weapons and forms of combat were employed, with the exception of the mysterious weapon that had struck the world with sudden fear in the recent African war; magical systems were only to appear at a later date.

In spite of the permanent contact of the parties, there were gaseous poisonings, insane microbial attacks, volleys of missiles and formidable artificial storms that destroyed the riches of a region, meridianist or parallelist, in a matter of minutes. Soon, however, some weapons, as dangerous to the assailant as to the targeted enemy, were virtually abandoned. Thus, microbial attacks were quickly renounced, as were toxic gases and long-range missiles, whose employment was unreliable by virtue of the multiplicity of energetic barrages.

The second period of the conflict began: an immense drama in which there were innumerable shifts of fortune, generally of brief duration: a sort of universal guerilla war, mingled with singular localized calms, during which appeals for justice, fraternal sermons and even vehement expostulations and terrible threats still made themselves heard.

The power-stations producing public energy and the zones of the central network—common riches that each party considered, not without reason, as the indispensable framework of modern civilization—were still spared: an empirical rule of the new game of war, dictated by a residue of prudence and, above all, the tenacious illusion that the troubles of the moment were only a temporary fever, after which humankind, rid of morbid impedimenta, would depart briskly toward a new destiny.

The majority of channels of communication thus remained open. They were little used, however, for the slightest journey by public transport, aerial or terrestrial, was a perilous enterprise. The vicinity of the major airports and railway stations, in particular, served continuously as battlefields.

There was, in any case, fighting everywhere, from the equator to the poles, on the ground, in the air, and even in the accessible layers of the oceans. There was fighting between neighbors, between one alignment and another—and the conflict sometimes then took on a singular aspect.

In certain somewhat isolated regions it was, in fact, not rare to see secondary rules, adapted to local circumstances, discreetly applied—with the consequence that the fighting was rather mild. A common desire for self-preservation tempered the ardor of the adversaries. There were tacit truces, periods of prudent expectation during which everyone waited for victory to crown the heroism of distant partisans. The fear of reprisals prevented the employment of the most advanced weapons, which would have destroyed not merely human beings but every manifestation of civilization. The frightful missile-launching pistols were sometimes replaced by antiques and enormous nitrogenous-powder machine-guns, which made a great deal of noise but did relatively little harm.

Vain prudence, alas!—for the danger not only came from the immediate neighborhood but from all points of the horizon.

In any case, any region in which people were fighting with economic courage, as if unwillingly, constituted an exception. Most of the time, the conflict between compatriots was atrocious. Both sides possessed an abundance of substances of capable of instantaneous disintegration. The violence of the explosions rendered all defense futile and the attacker was guaranteed an effective strike. The major alignments of the principal network were the first to crumble; then it was the turn of the isolated habitations built in irregular chaplets along the secondary lines. Destruction led to destruction; when the first house fell, the fate of the others was settled, without appeal; in a matter of hours, they disappeared.

In that strange war, underground shelters only offered an illusory security; the unprotected population dispersed between the zones and fled, in the invariable disappointed hope of landing on peaceful shores further away.

The extreme suffering did not calm hatred; the desire for vengeance set wandering groups that had nothing more to lose than life at one another's throats. Those who still had modern weapons created voids around them, and soon destroyed one another. Others, completely disarmed, fought like savages or wild beasts. In the depths of rural areas there were encounters in which strength and cunning resumed all their rights, encounters worthy of the age of cave-dwellers, in which the rage of the victors was slaked by the massacre of males.

The aerial war, universal and continuous, was even more murderous than the war on the ground. An immense flock of combat aircraft encircled the globe. Perhaps a hundred million machines had taken flight. Those attempting to flee were doubtless fairly numerous among the population of the air, but the most fanatical partisans were also to be found there: all the national militias poisoned by martial vanity, all the firebrands of the five continents, all the adventurers and pirates. There was no apparatus that was not armed. From that moving ceiling, lightning sprang forth continuously.

Free of all shackles, men of prey scoured the skies. Active, joyful and ferocious, devoid of shame or pity, as ready for any audacity as any treason, adventurers profited from the disorder to give free rein to their worst instincts. Unstoppable gangs tacked from one pole to the other, tracking the isolated, even attacking the half-empty expresses of the general network.

There were also operations on a vast scale. Leaders endowed with powerful arrogance, as carefree in the midst of the storm as large raptors, temporarily orientated the partisan mobs. Sudden assemblies formed, as if millions of aircraft had been seized by some mysterious field of force. In the night sky, immense squadrons passed like whirlwinds; growing by the second, they went at meteoric speed toward fatal encounters in which they ripped one another to shreds in an apocalyptic tumult. Great battles were fought in this way above Central America, Australia and the China Sea, and another—the most ferocious and the most terrible of all—above the north polar ice-cap, in the strange light of the aurora borealis: frightfully murderous battles, but indecisive, devoid of any tactical efficacy.

The conflict, conducted by ordinary methods, seemed bound to become eternal, or, at least, to last long enough for the total exhaustion of both parties, until all aircraft were destroyed and all the alignments sacked—

but the long-deferred intervention of the etheric physicists was to change the face of things even more radical-
ly than in the African war. Science, opening a period of
monstrous possibilities, was to bring about a rapid de-
nouement.

As soon as the first troubles erupted, the great
council of scientists had denounced the frightful risks
that humankind was about to run, but the voice of reason
was too weak and too cold to pierce the tumult of unleashed political passions. In any case, a number of scientists had themselves been rapidly drawn into the tragic
eddies. Although some of them, in the rare periods of
calm, tried to raise the cry of alarm, others, on the contrary, were improving known weapons and inventing
new ones in secret laboratories. They usually claimed, in
good faith, only to be trying to develop reliable and easily manipulative defensive weapons—weapons of terrible
protective power, the mere threat of which would quell
the fury of the malevolent.

Meteorologists, psychologists and chemists worked
feverishly, as did physicists of the modern school. The
latter studied magical systems with particular attention.
The problem no longer consisted of producing active
systems—that had been only too successful at the end of
the African war—but of limiting the area of dispersion
in a precise fashion, of orientating them exclusively to
follow either the parallels or the meridians.

The physicists of both parties found the solution,
and, unfortunately found it at almost the same moment.

It was, however, an intervention by meteorologists
that marked the entry of the war into its final phase. One
of their engineers, an Australian of the parallelist party,
had discovered a means of directing, at long distances,

invisible mists formed of extremely tiny and highly unstable corpuscles, whose instantaneous disintegration could be produced at will. After a few fruitless attempts, the Australians brought off a masterstroke. On a dark night, an immense meridianist squadron that was heading at top speed for the austral regions, where an enemy assembly had been spotted, ran into one of these strange clouds above the ocean. When all the machines had gone into the danger zone, the atmosphere exploded, along with the considerable quantities of radioactive substances transported by the squadron. The release of heat was considerable; fast-moving meteors reached the limits of the terrestrial atmosphere. The squadron had been annihilated in less than a second.

The world situation was too confused for the parallelist party to be able to proclaim its victory loudly. A few leaders, however, arrogating the right to speak in the name of all, called upon those they called "the rebels" to surrender immediately. The Australian engineer announced that he could also intervene, by an analogous process in the terrestrial war, and that, whenever he pleased, he could annihilate, methodically and without risk, all the meridianist alignments.

The immediate and terrible riposte came from an unknown laboratory. The arrogant demand of the parallelists had scarcely been issued than a magical invasion afflicted western Australia. The meridians remained immune, but the pullulating etheric systems followed the parallelist lines, reaching all the way to the ultimate ramifications of the secondary network.

In the same region, six hours later, a second magical appeared, this time striking the meridians to the exclusion of the parallels.

From then on, humankind lost control of its actions.

It did not seem that the insensate offensives that succeeded one another without respite and in all directions, launched by isolated physicists or low-ranking laboratory workers, could be attributed to the desire for vengeance or to martial vanity, or even political passion. They were, rather, gestures of panic, the violent reflexes of strong men, who, threatened with being stifled in the midst of a crowd in a location without exits, stampeded, trampling the weak for the derisory satisfaction of being the last to die. Maddened, their nerves overwrought, sensing terrible calamities descending upon hem, the unfortunates, pacifists until then, lashed out desperately, seeking to create a void around them by liberating the diabolical power of the new elements.

Throughout the world, there was a continuous eruption of magicals. Thousands of systems, visible or invisible, populated the zones, selecting, in accordance with the initial contact, the parallels or the meridians.

A few, of restricted range, only exercised their influence in the immediate vicinity of the lines, but others emitted radiations of considerable power. That radiation, which almost always created tumultuous colonies within the human body, presented characteristics so variable that any general measure was derisory in its futility. Even the etheric specialists could not protect themselves effectively.

Again, according to the region, people were afflicted by mortal dermatitis, monstrous neoplasms, the strangest nervous disruptions and other ill-effects worst still. Unprecedented afflictions, hectically varied, descended upon humankind.

In Australia, a part of the parallel population was reducing to crawling; the principal effect of the radiation of the first magical had been a considerable and almost instantaneous softening of the skeleton. The limbs, swollen at the extremities, stretched like strips of rubber. The upper body was compacted or elongated; even the head became as malleable as a slack blister.

On the other hand, in the same region, a large number of the inhabitants of the meridians had been congealed by the radiation of the second magical; thousands of cadavers, dry and sonorous, had fallen to the ground simultaneously.

In Japan, grave disturbances were observed originating from the motor nerve-centers. In some cantons the entire population was staggering. Among the least afflicted, gestures were disordered. The simplest grasping actions often became impossible; the hands slid over objects or, by contrast, clenched avidly upon empty space. Many seemed to have lost the most elementary notion of extent; starving individuals were seen lying on the ground, impetuously raising their hands toward tempting fruits at the top of a tree but considering with sadly forlorn eyes, as if they were out of range, the nourishment that was placed in front of their lips.

A few intact alignments in southern India sheltered the death-throes of delirious paralytics. Also paralytic, but lucid, were the inhabitants of the Formosan parallels. The inhabitants of the meridians, afflicted by magical rabies, wandered the island in haggard and howling bands, hurling themselves on their immobile adversaries and biting them as dogs might have done.

The Persians of an overpopulated general alignment became hairy, clawed and prodigiously nymphomaniac in a matter of hours; as if an invincible force were driving them to fatal embraces, they agglutinated in swarms and stifled one another, gurgling with fury.

Blind, phosphorescent and exhilarated Chileans dug down vertically in the friable parts of the ground without respite, until they were buried head-down.

In Central America, small groups of sentimental and neurasthenic cannibals encountered one another; Mexicans wept as they gnawed the skulls of their children, after having plucked out all the hair with minute care and infinite tenderness.

At numerous points of the European alignments, the inhabitants, even those who seemed unafflicted, could not resist the temptation to gorge themselves on filthy nourishment.

Among the Siberians, where simple dermatitis had already caused frightful ravages, the flesh was also seen to split, enormous fissures reaching the essential organs without leading to immediate death, or the skin became flaccid, hanging in vast elastic festoons that soon fused together at points of contact.

Five million Chinese on the Yunnam parallel suddenly acquired bones as brittle as glass; the unfortunates perished after a short time after atrocious suffering, their skeletons shattered and their flesh tortured by fragments.

Their Tonkinese adversaries of the meridian alignments suffered a disgrace of the same nature, but even more complete and sinister. Their limbs were desiccated, as if they had been exposed to the fire of a kiln for a long time. The affliction began in the lower extremities and rapidly reached the major muscular masses; the arms were the last to be attained. The dead organs broke or crumbled at the slightest shock but the rest of the body continued nevertheless to live. To these atrocious afflictions was added a jovial and noisy madness. The unfortunate could be seen lying on the threshold of their houses, throwing fragments of toenails, knucklebones or shreds of calves rolled into balls and masticated at their own heads, with mischievous expressions. Legless individuals broke their hardened phalanges like twigs and amused themselves by eating them, laughing wholeheartedly and sarcastically.

Some magicals of restricted range exercised a completely different action on psychic life. Far from provoking an instantaneous mental degeneration, they excited the faculties of imagination or reason. Veils were torn away; an abrupt enlightenment dissipated mists. Touched by the radiation, humble individuals were elevated at a stroke to the level of the greatest thinkers. The honey of an incomparable poetry flowed from the lips of the illuminati. Those who were not ill heard with delight and amazement the tones of an unknown eloquence. Ancient problems, hitherto deemed to be insoluble, were suddenly resolved with a supernatural facility.

That magnificent exaltation did not last long, and was, unfortunately, always accompanied by serious physiological disturbances. Uncontrollable tremors, general paralyses and epileptic crises of increasing violence, rapidly terminated by death, were the most common sequels. In Cuba, following the 80 meridian, several hundred mulattos among whom the most powerful philosophical genius had awakened, had simultaneously lost all aptitude for walking normally, and nevertheless could not remain still. Nuclei of tumultuous life infused their limbs with an extreme irritability of considerable force. Prolonged contact with the ground was a torture for them; they leapt about like grasshoppers until they were completely exhausted.

Often, among those minds were stimulated, there was a simultaneous degeneration of the sensory organs. Blindness was the rule, deafness frequent. The abolition

of the senses of taste, smell and even touch were sometimes added. Mathematicians, philosophers or poets for a
day, who had reached heights never attained before with
miraculous ease, thus went through a final strange stage
before dying, passing into a sort of nirvana in which only certain regions of their consciousness remained alive
and prodigiously active.

When death was delayed, the formation of replace-
ment organs was observed. In the middle of the forehead, on the nape of the neck or along the vertebral column, beneath the skin, which had become transparent,
rudimentary eyes appeared. Invalids were not uncom-
mon who could no longer hear with their ears but with
the palms of their hands, which had become insensitive
to touch. In others, deprived of the five ordinary senses,
certain tegumentary formations acquired a universal sensitivity. Reacting simultaneously to the action of sound,
light, electrical or psychic waves, these new organs furnished the brain with a spectrum of information that was
undoubtedly confused but extremely varied.

Tripolitan poets, blind and deaf but with foreheads
embellished with slender retractile tentacles, navigated
with the surety of homing pigeons.

Domestic personnel in the British isles, mutated into metaphysicians, had bodies covered in fine golden
fleeces reminiscent of the down of ducklings, the thousand tiny antennae of which captured the most subtle
psychic radiations as they passed.

Others attracted lightning; others became radioactive, and exploded after a few hours; others became ven-
omous, and simple contact with them was fatal.

One of the most formidable and surprising successes was a magical system that propagated all around the
northern hemisphere following the fortieth degree of

latitude: an invisible system formed by a crown of minuscule regradatory vortices uniformly distributed along the axis of the energetic zone. It did not have any gross physiological effect and its existence would have gone unperceived had there not been observed at the same moment, in more than a million people, strange perturbations of the memory. Two symmetrical segments could be distinguished in the etheric crown, in which the radiation had diametrically opposed effects.

Among the yellows of the Asiatic segment, the visual memory had completely disappeared. The afflicted members of the same family no longer recognized one another, nor could they recognize their homeland, their house or the objects that surrounded them, any more than they could recognize the organs of their own body. All that was new to them; they lived in perpetual astonishment and perpetual agitation. After a few days or a few hours, madness ensued, ordinarily preceded by violent crises of terror. The scourge attained its greatest intensity among the Chinese on either side of the 260 meridian.

In the idle of the opposite segment, among the American of the 40.80 region, the memory was, by contrast, stimulated. A host of extinct memories welled up simultaneously and in the same plane: memories of individual life and memories emerging from the distant past of the species. The invalids remained transfixed by stupor before that prodigious flourishing of images and sensations. They sensed their personality dissolve. They were lost in a boundless forest, among unusual foliage, animated by magical breezes. Floating motionless above a phantasmagorical ocean, they saw gliding toward hem, vertiginously, from the depths of the inexhaustible horizon, the previously-glimpsed shores of familiar isles, and, in thousands, white and ponderous vessels inflating their sails with the black wind of the ages, whose hulls were lining up side by side in a sudden dazzling light. And the victims, through that immense and tremulous halo, rapidly arrived in the harbors of death.

At progressively greater distances from the 40.80 point, the center of the positive segment, the effect of the magical radiation on the memory became more selective. Among the Americans of the West and the Europeans, the disturbance was no longer general. Some memories surged forth individually, violently illuminated between two zones of shadow. Ordinarily, that singular revivification brought back into the light not memories of individual life—they, on the contrary, retreated to the point of being utterly effaced—but memories several centuries old, or even images of an infinitely more opaque past, from which no light had ever seemed able to return.

These memories immediately organized themselves into logically admissible systems and imposed themselves on the mind as the only actual realities. The past, with a brutal shove, rejected the present from consciousness. Thus were effected veritable ancestral reincarnations.

The Americans of Utah, in whom the adventurous soul of Christian conquistadors of the sixteenth century was revived, decked themselves with tawdry ornaments and barbaric weapons, and departed in search of discoveries. All personal memory having vanished, nothing happened to break the enchantment. They plunged into the unknown land, marveling at every step, but without fear. When they encountered natives speaking a language they did not understand. They fell upon them, and they thought about the tales they would tell on their return: magnificent tales that no one would believe, about the paradise of flying humans, living vehicles and a thousand other fabulous things.

Some Iberians of Baixo Mondego, only taken back twelve centuries, set off to war against the heretic dogs of the Emperor Napoléon. They set ambushes in orchards, on the edges of roads, and, as every passer-by had the face of a foreigner, they killed them pitilessly.

A Greek with a determined expression had his slaves whipped. He was a common-law criminal and the slaves expert psychologists from a house of correction, who allowed themselves to be beaten without raising the slightest protest.

Not far away, a famous philosopher of the modern school, whose antiquated body was animated by the mind of an Alexandrian courtesan, decorated his flesh-less shoulders with flowers and inscribed the price of a night of pleasure on the wall of his house.

The Sardinians touched by the radiation were taken back to ages more distant still, and social forms scarcely suspected. The most civilized, grouped in small tribes, chipped flints and supervised with jealous concern the living flower of flame. They had a rudimentary but articulate language. The males invited one another to fight by striking their breasts and imitating the roaring of wild beasts. The women knew how to smile; among the dancing lights of big fires, they sketched rhythmic capers, miming the cadenced gestures of love.

Other primitives, much coarser, armed their fists with sticks and lumpen stones. They made simply-agglutinated guttural sounds; no smiles softened the faces of the women, and the adults neither played nor danced. Silent lake-dwellers huddled in the reeds of banks. Tree-dwelling howlers climbed into the tops of trees, where they built rounded huts covered with roofs of foliage with an astonishing dexterity; they searched for fruits and tender shoots, and gnawed the bark of young trees avidly.

A few groups manifested frank aggression; others did not seek combat, but at the slightest sign of danger came together, growling and ready for confrontation. On the other hand, numerous individuals were found who were completely devoid of gregarious instinct. They usually fled in alarm at any threat, and refused any prolonged effort. Their peers, in very remote times, had probably populated vast regions of the planet. In singular, highly unfavorable circumstances analogous in some ways to the present circumstances, in which warlike gestures presented the worst dangers, the survival of the species had doubtless only been assured by the dispersal of groups, the prudence of individuals and their extreme simplicity.

Finally, strange people were encountered with sad and docile eyes, humans who were very docile but anxious and disorientated, like domesticated birds released from their cages. They seemed to be in search of masters, in quest of care, caresses and orders. Their presence rendered Roume's hypothesis admissible. They doubtless resuscitated the contemporaries of the fabulous creatures who had disappeared mysteriously in the Tertiary Era; they were the domestic companion of those demigods, of whom, thanks to the subtle resources of modern science, confused traces were believed to have been recovered in the depths of the Pacific Ocean in the vicinity of Easter Island.

Twenty days after the appearance of the first etheric system in Australia, only three or four hundred million people in reasonably good health could be counted.

The insanity was at its peak. All groups were breaking up. Some individuals, their capacity for suffering surpassed, no longer reacted. Consciousness was overturned by the wind of the horrible; cases of spontaneous insanity and suicides multiplied among the unafflicted population.

Almost all labor had been suspended. The central power-stations were, however, still functioning. Stoically, their minds closed, clinging to their duty as the only stable reality, a few dozen engineers, disseminated over the planet, kept watch on the sacred fire, maintaining the power of modern humankind for the uncertain future of the race. Formidable dynamos, set up for several months of operation, were still sending torrents of energy around the world.

Their brutal stoppage, causing the destruction of the zones, would certainly have disarmed people to a great extent, but, on the other hand, it was a difficult and hazardous enterprise. A general famine would inevitably follow; the world would be plunged back into full barbarity for a long time. No international authority existed any longer; no one, at any rate, would have been able to coordinate the acts of destruction that might perhaps have been acts of salvation.

On the twentieth day of the magical war, several power-stations nevertheless shut down, in consequence of unknown circumstances. The diminution of energy in the secondary zones was evident. At the same time, the great human disorder seemed to die down; there was an astonishing calm.

It was the singular hour in which destiny hesitated.

The cinetelephonic organization had suffered serious damage, and the General News was no longer informing the crowds. Numerous items of private apparatus were, however, still functioning.

On the twenty-first day, at ten o'clock in the morning on the original meridian, after a few minutes of strange silence, all the receivers began to resonate in an unexpected fashion. Disorderly clamors from all directions overlapped. They did not take long to become organized—and there was something suggestive of the immense plaint of the Earth, and then a heart-rending appeal, and then an urgent plea laden with menace, which flew toward Western Europe, the land of the great laboratories, finally focusing on *The Refuge*.

"Harrisson! Harrisson! Save us! Break the weapons in the murderers' hands! You alone can act! You must act! Quickly! Quickly! You were the creator of the diabolical forces! Break the insane circle of our misery! Time is passing; the storm will gather again above our heads! And you aren't responding! The blood of the dead cries out against you, bringer of curses! Harrisson! Perhaps it's not too late! Harrisson! Harrisson! Save humankind!"

Harrisson was not at *The Refuge*. The previous day, on Lygie's insistence, he had left his house to go to the 4.48 laboratory, where a few of the most celebrated scientists were already in conference: Roume, the ex-chief power-station engineer Norrès, the Japanese Takase and three Americans.

Harrisson had brought his colleagues bad news. Not only had he not glimpsed any possibility of stopping the magical invasion without destroying all the zones, but, confirming certain observations already made by Takase, he announced that secondary systems had appeared spontaneously on several occasions outside the energy zones. This was not surprising, for it was now possible to produce diffuse magical systems, to whose radiation all points of the Earth would be exposed.

Still an advocate of the immediate destruction of the power-stations, Harrisson no longer dared believe in the complete efficacy of that desperate remedy. He even wondered whether the sudden disappearance of that energy might lead to the rupture of the mysterious equilibrium and an unexpected recrudescence of spontaneous formations.

They had, however, tried once more to make the voice of reason heard. For more than twelve hours, the scientists had been broadcasting on the cinetelephone, begging any international authorities that might still exist to pull themselves together. They had attempted a supreme appeal to the personnel of laboratories, all the scientists of the planet, their aides, assistants and families.

The most urgent exhortations were lost in the tumult.

In truth, all hope had been abandoned at the 4.48 when the miraculous calm developed, when the rumor of distress coming from all parts of the Earth rose up, increasing by the minute.

"Harrison! Save your brethren!"

Harrisson made no reply. He knew how chimerical the hope was that they were investing in him. Science could no longer save civilization. For several days now, he had seen his most pessimistic anticipations surpassed. The consciousness of his impotence was crushing him, along with the consciousness of his distant responsibility.

"Harrisson! Hurry up! Time is pressing! We're going to die!"

He consulted his colleagues with his gaze. Motionless, Takase still had his thin smile. The others came closer, gathering around the Master. "Show yourself and speak!" they said.

Ravaged with anguish, like him, paler after each clamor, they repeated: "Show yourself and talk to the people!"

"What can I tell them that hasn't already been said? Haven't your words been in vain?"

"It's you they're calling for!" they replied. "They're putting their confidence in you alone!"

Then one of the Americans said, in a breathless and brutal voice: "Speak—for among us, you're the most guilty."

Harrisson still hesitated. The others around him offered their contradictory advice, feverishly.

"Be the dictator!"

"Get the principal leaders of the meridianists and parallelists together!"

"Have the zones destroyed!"

"No!"

"We have to save the zones."

"No!"

"Speak!"

"Order!"

"Judge!"

"Condemn!"

Harrison shook his head. "I'll simply lie," he said. "Let's try to create peace by announcing it. Perhaps, that way, there's a slight chance of salvation. If we can gain time...! Come with me, then and support my lies."

They all went to the universal transmitter and sent out a signal advertising their presence. Soon, the distant cries died down. The dolor, the hatred and the fear fell silent; the somber group of scientists appeared on thousands of screens.

Harrison stepped forward and, in a firm and confident voice, hurling each syllable like a stone, he spoke.

"In the name of the physicists of the 4.48 laboratory, I, Harrisson, announce to everyone that the evil has been vanquished. The evil has been vanquished! The war is over!"

"Aah! Aah! Speak! Speak!"

Considerably muffled by the volume control, an immense rumor unfurled in the room. Harrisson raised his hand and silence fell again. Forcefully, he went on: "The war is over! The frightful danger that was facing humankind has been averted. Everyone keep calm. No one need hide any longer. Let no man raise his hand against his brother, either to attack or to defend himself...because the war is over. We're going to make war impossible. We're bringing you peace."

"Peace! Peace! Peace!" The word flowed like a divine caress over the agonized face of the Earth. All violence seemed to yield; the day became smooth again.

Harrisson felt a flickering flame of hope ignite in his heart, and he continued, with the slow gestures of a magician, the healing incantation:

"Look to us. Listen to our voice. Let those who can hear us spread the good news. After long research, we've found the sovereign remedy. We've dispelled the magical terror forever. We're giving the world peace and security. For several hours, now, the weapon has fallen from the hands of madmen and evildoers. If they try to take it up again, we shall punish them before the complete the action; they will be the first and only victims. There are no more evildoers. There are no more madmen. The war is over. Everyone is safe!"

He paused for a minute. The breath of the crowds took the form of confused acclamations, and sighs of relief and ecstasy.

"Peace! Peace! We want to live! Talk to us! Be our guide!"

With a gesture, he demanded silence again.

"We, the physicists of the 4.48, accept the role of your temporary council. Look to us. Listen carefully. The hour of madness has passed; the world is bright again. Have confidence! Let everyone return to their posts, peacefully, make gestures of peace, find peace once again in their souls. The laboratories still standing must be abandoned immediately. The imprudent individuals who remain there will be risking a frightful death; it will not be possible for us to save them. The power-station workers who have remained valiantly at their posts until today, must also leave the dynamos and put themselves in communication with the 4.48. They will receive personal instructions from chief engineer Norrès. Our discovery requires a complete overhaul of the general network indispensable. Let no one be alarmed about this; the new organization will be infinitely superior to the old; it will ensure the security and the surprising facility of life. Have confidence! An era of joy is about to commence. Men of good will, look to us! Misunderstandings will be dissipated. There will no longer be hatred between the parties. The new organization will bring the entire world into agreement; its order will be established naturally, without the weak ever being hurt. All people will enjoy happiness…and, finally, justice. Justice will reign!"

Harrison piled up the crazy promises, evoking the delights of a fabulous paradise. In the meantime, Norrès had gone to another apparatus and was preparing to send out the order to stop the power-stations—which would, for a time that would doubtless be long, reduce humankind to impotence.

The rumor of the planet was about to die down. As an invalid falls delightfully asleep after some frightful agony, the world seemed to be slipping into a reparative torpor.

Harrisson was still talking. He affirmed imperiously, careless of plausibility, instinctively finding the great beneficent lies and hypnotic gestures. His statements, mysteriously resonant and profound, passed like magnetic waves over breathless humankind. Untiringly, he repeated: "I bring you peace! I, Harrisson, order you to be confident. Look to us! Listen to what we say. Security is assured. The weapons are broken. Brother is embracing brother. The war is over. Justice will reign forever."

Suddenly, a clamor of terror, coming from the most distant regions of the Earth, emerged from the receivers: "The evil is upon us! Treason! Treason!"

The Japanese, in the next room, activated an ultra-rapid exploration apparatus, and announced: "A magical over China...parallels 36 and 37, with extension to the secondary network."

The scientists had gone pale. Roume and the Americans surrounded Norrès. The latter, feverishly, sent in all directions, without any encryption, the order to switch off the power-stations immediately. He insisted on the urgency, recommended the most rapid, violent and imprudent means.

Left alone, Harrisson, stiffening, resumed his speech: "Let no one be alarmed! A final ordeal has just struck our brothers in Asia. It was foreseen. We, the physicists of the 4.48, order once again that all laboratories be abandoned immediately."

A second clamor rent the air, and then the echo of a mighty explosion was heard.

"A magical over Ireland," the observer announced. "Meridian zone. A power-station exploded in Java."

"A power-station exploded!" Roume and the Americans repeated—and they pressed around Norrès, full of anguish.

"Quickly! Quickly!"

"Order everyone!"

"No more hesitation!"

"Destroy the power-stations, at all costs!"

In spite of the volume control, a storm of cries drowned out their voices.

"Harrisson has betrayed the parallelists! Death to Harrisson! Death!"

Then another, even more violent, rose up in the opposite direction.

"Harrisson has betrayed the meridianists! Death to Harrisson! Death to the physicists of the 4.48! A curse upon the scientists!"

Soon, there was a continuous, inexhaustible racket of jeers, punctuated by howls of hatred, suffering and terror.

"Death to Harrisson!"

"Treason!"

"The evil is upon us!"

"Treason!"

"Treason!"

Harrisson tried to continue the struggle. Standing firm, he spoke into the tumult.

"My life belongs to you! You will judge me! But one last time, listen to the orders of the 4.48. Salvation can come from here alone!"

Roume and the Americans, abandoning Norrès, surrounded Harrisson again, shouting.

"Destroy the power-stations!"

"Destroy the dynamos!"

"Blow up all the private laboratories!"

Meanwhile, the Japanese continued, in a louder voice: "Magical over India...parallel zones... Magical over Bavaria...meridian zones... Intersecting zones over Spain... Suspect the existence of an invisible system in easterly direction toward the 0.48 point...in our colleague Harrisson's neighborhood... Power-station exploded..."

Roume and the Americans were howling.

"Bravo!"

"Destroy the power-stations!"

"Destroy!"

"Destroy them all!"

"...Magical in the mid-North Atlantic... Magical over Yeso...my family doubtless struck...ah! Here's something interesting! Above Holland, a luminous sheet developing outside the zones... Gentlemen, I believe that we're in the presence of a spontaneous system, a belated echo of a magical extinct for several hours. Harrisson, my dear colleague, unless I'm mistaken, there's a remarkable subject of observation here..."

"Death! Death!" cried the entire world.

The Japanese resumed: "Magical over Switzerland... Complete silence in the Massif Central... Furious mob climbing toward *The Refuge*... Communication interrupted...zone of silence...black zone...ah! Finally!"

"What is it?" cried Roume.

"Gentleman, I no longer have eyes. Hearing is gradually disappearing too...quite quickly, it seems to me..."

The sound of a fall was heard.

"Gentlemen, I no longer have legs..."

They all ran. The Japanese was lying at the foot of the apparatus. They went to him and touched him.

Then, still calm, still smiling, he said: "Intersecting systems overhead. I suspect that they've been developing for several hours already. Undoubtedly, gentlemen, you're about to be afflicted, in a matter of minutes, as I have been. Nothing but the banal, in sum...apart from the Dutch magical...our colleague Harrison ought to study that...if he still has time..."

Harrisson was no longer listening. Leaning over the apparatus, he located *The Refuge*. He saw the intact house, the surrounding parkland, the neighboring power-station. Suddenly, however, between the plane-trees of the highway, a haggard mob emerged: fifty men and women with bloodshot eyes, who seemed to be impelled by fury...

Harrison stood up, livid. At his feet, Takase was dying. He stepped over him, and ran toward the exit. The others also tried to flee. One of the Americans stumbled and fell face down. Norrès and Roume, blinded, collided violently. Thrown against a wall, Roume continued to move in a straight line, pushing with his head and shoulders and howling.

Two Americans and Harrisson reached the door of the laboratory; there, the Americans collapsed. Harrison was still standing. His aircraft was twenty meters away, on a small take-off platform. He took four steps toward it, and felt himself totter. He fell on to his knees, rolled over on his side...

Then he started to crawl. He could no longer hear anything. There was an atrocious burning sensation at the back of his eyes. He could still see, however, as if through a mist, the nearest objects. He reached the platform and, with an immense effort, succeeded in sliding into the apparatus.

His fingers touched the controls.

Like an arrow, the aircraft lifted off obliquely, in the direction of 0.48.

IV. Blind Fury

The dancer Sylvia climbed up toward *The Refuge*, leading fifty lunatics.

The previous day, Lahorie, afflicted by the radiation of a magical, had died in the uniform of domestic personnel, in a crisis of furious madness. She, less gravely afflicted, had temporarily escaped dementia, but had nevertheless found herself prey to a very violent excitement. Throwing away the vulgar vestments of a kitchen-maid, in which she had been disguised since the African war, she had put on the sumptuous tunic of a queen of love, had ornamented herself with marvelous jewels, and then, incapable of staying still, had set out for adventure, laughing, weeping, dancing and singing.

The clamor of hatred raised against Harrisson had struck her ears, and immediately, under the impact, the old wound to her self-esteem had begun to bleed again. Her excitement had found a direction; a furious desire for vengeance had filled her soul.

She had added her voice to the other delirious voices, and then had set out for *The Refuge*. She had arrived alone at the 0.48 power-station. There, a recent magical of limited but very variable action, had just claimed victims. Numerous cadavers were lying on the ground, and paralytics dragging themselves along on their knees and elbows. Blind people, their orbits half-empty and their facial muscles twitching, were running in all directions, hands forward, offering their frightful burns to the coolness of the breeze.

All the wounded were crying treason.

Sylvia had thrown herself into the midst of the blind people, whipping up their wrath with her voice—and soon, grouped behind her, they had set out for *The Refuge*...

Sylvia marched at the head of the column, her right arm raised, her eyes full of flames. Three blind men hung on to the floating fabric of her tunic; the others followed, staggering. Her appeals rang out; she infused her wretched companions with all her hatred.

"Anyone who doesn't come with me is a coward! Harrisson has betrayed you, as he has betrayed me, as he has betrayed all of humankind! Let him die under torture! Follow me! We'll crush the beast, we'll burn his lair!"

Her excitement increased by the minute, almost approaching veritable madness. The blind people clustered in the wake of her violence. Howls of fury drowned out the moans of agony, cries of despair and the outbursts of laughter of the intoxicated and delirious.

"A curse upon Harrisson! Let him die! Let him feel our knees on his breast, our fingernails in his flesh, in his eyes...!"

They reached *The Refuge*. Old Salem appeared on the threshold of the house. Terrified, he said: "Go away! The person you're looking for isn't here."

A volley of cries drowned him out.

"Death to Harrisson and his household! Vengeance!"

The old man tried to retreat, but did not have time. Already, Sylvia had leapt upon him and shoved him toward the blind people. The nearest ones grabbed hold of him. He fell to the ground, dragging two of his tormentors with him. The others followed the sound; several stumbled. Those who were still standing trampled those who had fallen, striking at hazard with forceful thrusts of their heels and ferocious grunts. A woman with a horrible, flayed face had bitten Salem's throat like a she-wolf; blood from the carotid was still splashing her hair. An adolescent, drunk on exhilarants, coughed as he plunged his thumbs into the cadaver's eyes.

At that moment, Lygie came out of the subterranean laboratory where, for an hour, full of anguish, with her eyes riveted to the cinetelephone, she had been following Harrisson's last strange attempt. It had required the shouts of the assailants to get very close for her to understand what was happening and decide to go upstairs.

When she appeared at the entrance to the vestibule, Sylvia was searching the house. Guided by her furious voice, blind people were groping along the walls, trying to catch up with her. Others, persevering in the assault on Salem's cadaver and those of their own companions, were tearing one another apart hideously.

Confronted by that hideous spectacle, Lygie remained nailed to the spot. A blind man, running and howling, brushed past her—and all of a sudden she screamed too, frantic with horror. An abrupt anguish had cut through her like a blade; in a flash, she had a vision of a frightful danger. That very morning, hoping against all hope, had she not applied the creative stimulus once again? The marvelous apparatus was functioning, carefully isolated from the public zones; it would only require some brutal shock, the action of an imprudent, ignorant, insane individual, to put the laboratory in communication with the outside world—and then, system 13 would expand over the Earth with a facility of which the invasions of primitive magicals could give no idea. Sterilizing nuclei would form instantaneously throughout the telluric ether...

At all costs, it was necessary to prevent access to the laboratory, and, with the necessary precautions, to destroy the apparatus.

Lygie launched forward...but a demented scream rose up behind her; before she had taken three steps, two hands seized her shoulders.

Sylvia, perceiving her rival, had pounced.

"To me!" she cried. "We'll have our vengeance!"

In response to her voice, those who were strangling one another and tearing one another apart let go; those who were rolling on the ground got to their feet; almost all the blind rallied. The howling of wild beasts filled the vestibule.

Lygie had sufficient strength to turn round, and her voice rose up in the tumult, simultaneously pleading and threatening.

"Don't come any further! There's mortal danger— and worse! Terrible danger...for all humankind!"

Hands clenched around her throat. In the semi-darkness, close to her face, she saw the ardent face of Sylvia—and she saw, a little behind, the red and empty eyes and black mouths howling for death. The demonic breath of a dog-pack hurling itself at its prey enveloped her like a flame.

Mad with fear, she tried again to get away. With a desperate effort, she dragged Sylvia and the two blind men clinging to her shoulders. She reached the laboratory. On the experimental bench, almost within arm's reach, a weapon had been placed by Harrisson: a blasting pistol, aimed at the laboratory entrance. Perhaps salvation! Already, she was reaching out...

But she felt fingernails digging further into her flesh; she lost her breath, stumbled...

The human cluster fell to the floor.

The blind people arrived. The first, shoved by those who were following, fell in their turn. Lygie was choking, tramped by feet, her throat caught in a vice, an enormous weight on her breast.

"Vengeance! Vengeance!" cried the blind.

A man with a bloody face, a giant shaking with the atrocious laughter of the intoxicated, had found a heavy steel rod under his hand. He whirled it around his head, striking out randomly.

The howls of pain and rage were redoubled. Suddenly, Sylvia fell silent, her skull split. Lygie, half-dead, vaguely felt the grip of the ferocious fingers relax. She was hardly suffering any longer. Sylvia's blood ran over her face; she turned her head, coughing. Her lips opened; a little air entered her pressurized lungs, a little life...

Then, an immense dolor awakened; a horrible black flood submerged her soul. Before her rolled-back eyes, the lightning of the rod had sprung forth.

The big blind barbarian shattered the safety-bells and smashed the insulators.

System 13 invaded the world.

Human destiny was about to be accomplished. It was the end of all joy and all suffering, the irremediable misfortune...death.

"Death! Death!"

The word expired on Lygie's violet lips. She received a blow on the head and lost consciousness.

The blind man was still lashing out. Around him, everyone within the range of his arm had fallen. The survivors were flooding back into the vestibule. There was a little click, and then a sinister hiss, and soft bodies crumbled. The rod had just collided with the aimed weapon. The pistol spat out its thunderbolt.

A sudden silence fell. Only the blind mass-murderer was still standing. A fresh breeze struck his agonized face. Sobered up, he became anxious.

"Brothers, where are you?"

The unexpected silence chilled him. Breathlessly, he repeated: "Brothers, where are you? Where am I, brothers? Brothers!"

Then, behind him, a strange, inhuman plaint suddenly went up: a feeble quaver of distress that seemed to come from a very long way away, rising from some mysterious abyss.

Fear ran down the man's spine. He dropped his weapon and bounded in the direction of the air-current. Trampling bodies, falling, and then getting up again, he reached the exit and ran away, half-mad, his hands trembling, groping in the darkness.

Behind the insulating curtain, huddled at the back of their playroom, Samuel and Flore, holding one another tightly, were sobbing, on a high and tremulous note.

At an altitude of a thousand meters, scarcely a minute after his departure from the 4.48, Harrisson found that he was completely blind and deaf, and noticed too that his fingers were having difficulty maintaining contact with objects. His legs dead, he was sprawled in the narrow monoplane, his right hand on the control lever.

His mind remained agile, but was working in an unexpected fashion, as if it had been enriched by mysterious new resources.

The aircraft, headed in the direction of *The Refuge*, entered a strong transversal current and was carried slightly northwards. Immediately, a dolorous frisson ran through the pilot's fingers; he leaned to the right. His movement had the rapidity of a reflex.

The pain ceased, and Harrisson had the certainty of steering his aircraft more surely than he had been able to do by sight.

With his left hand, which was still free, he searched for one of the forward portholes. Through the narrow opening, his fingers groped in the void. He did not feel the freshness of the wind on his skin but, on the contrary, a slight burning sensation that would have astonished him a hour earlier, but which now seemed perfectly natural.

His fingers parted, slowly orientating themselves without the intervention of his will—and little by little, the darkness into which he had been plunged was populated by fantastic apparitions.

What he was able to distinguish below him bore no resemblance to the banal forms of the world. No ordinary glimmers delimited contours—and yet, it was not chaos. New sensations, instantaneously elaborated, procured him strange certainties that concerned neither space nor time, as they were humanly conceivable, but which were applicable to a mysterious and formidable entity behind mobile illusion.

His thoughts were seething, dilating infinitely. He was suffering confusedly. He had the impression that he was at the dolorous heart of the world, and that unknown vibrations were converging on him from every direction.

A few sensations became more precise. A narrow, sharp, human suffering pierced his vague anguish like a ray of light; he entered into communication with Lygie. He lived the horrible scene, perceived the fury of the attackers, Sylvia's dementia; pointed fingernails throttled him; his chest caved in, he croaked...

Then an indescribable horror made every fiber of his being quiver...

Finally, a blow to the head plunged him, for a few seconds, into complete darkness...

The aircraft fell.

Suddenly, it righted itself and climbed almost vertically, at great speed.

His hand clenching the control lever, Harrisson fled the land of sterile humankind. All suffering concentrated in his heart once again, he fled the Earth, from which an immense and unanimous rumor of curses rose up toward him.

He completed his dying in the vertiginous deserts of the sky, in the din of a explosive disintegration. There was a great devouring flame. Heavy gases and ashes descended slowly, to mingle with the clouds.

PART THREE: A GENESIS

I. Sterile Humanity

Humankind did not understand, at first, that it had received the *coup de grâce*.

The formation of the various magicals had recommenced. Spontaneous formations were evolving all over the world; thus, system 13 had invaded the world without anyone manifesting any particular alarm. Among so many dramatic manifestations succeeding one another without respite, the abortions could not attract special attention. Besides which, cinetelephonic communications were becoming increasing difficult and precarious; the universality of the scourge had not even been noticed.

The final episode of the tragedy unfolded in bleak horror. Belatedly obedient to the instruction from the 4.48, people destroyed the power-stations, the zones, the laboratories and even the reserves of radioactive substances patiently accumulated in the course of several centuries.

Either because the destruction was too abrupt, however, or because an unsuspected equilibrium had been broken, or for some other reason, the disturbance of the telluric ether persisted. It was only after ten days that the world recovered its accustomed stability and the last magical disappeared.

Civilization had foundered. With the exception of a few rare aircraft and a few private cinetelephonic installations virtually everything that had comprised the power and pride of modern society disappeared. Furthermore, the world was depopulated. Perhaps a hundred million people remained, seemingly unafflicted. Two or three times as many, the victims of the last magicals, were ending their lives atrociously. Vast regions were littered with moaning paralytics dying of hunger and thirst; in other places, scarcely anyone could be found who was not blind. Crazed and hallucinated individuals, and monsters who no longer had human faces, were wandering aimlessly. None of the social groups had survived. Only a few families still existed. Individuals procured their subsistence from day to day, living in a perpetual state of alert.

The infirm and the mentally disturbed disappeared rapidly. A month after the destruction of the power-stations, tranquility reigned over the devastated Earth. The survivors undertook humble enterprise, silently organizing their new existence. Life was primitive, prudent and economical.

The lethargy was not to last, however. A muted anxiety took hold of the more clear-sighted. Some physicians now recalled the strange series of abortions doubtless caused by the magical invasion. Each one, within his radius of observation, was able to observe that no children were being born, that there was no expectation of any, and no prospect for the future.

The malaise was rapidly amplified. The last cinetelephonic installations were employed feverishly; the last aircraft took off to carry out research—and the anguishing certainty as soon acquired that the evil extended over the entire Earth. People still wanted to believe, however, that it was a temporary and curable affliction. Physicians and biologists who had, miraculously, saved some of their scientific equipment, began a minute examination of their own sexual organs and those of their neighbors. Everywhere, the results were identical: everyone—men, women and children of both sexes—seemed to be irremediably sterile.

The scientists were unable to keep the terrible news secret for long. Anguish gripped their entourages; even strangers ran to them demanding imperiously to be examined.

Soon, via the cinetelephone and aircraft, and also by virtue of some mysterious intuition, everyone was informed. The truth burst upon the world like an epidemic. The species was condemned to die.

The enormity of the sentence crushed humankind.

To be sure, they had just gone through a period of immense misfortunes, had been subjected to terrible suffering; all that nevertheless remained admissible, for it had only been a question of the more or less rapid disappearance of individuals. This time, however, the well of life had run dry at a stroke. It was a catastrophe of an entirely unaccustomed kind, a unique catastrophe that surpassed understanding. The collapse was, therefore, complete. The deaths of innumerable individuals had merely disaggregated social groups; the simple announcement of the disappearance of the species immediately dislocated minds.

The spirit of enterprise was immediately snuffed out. The humble projects commenced were abandoned. Even among the coarsest and most backward of humans, and the half-mad, who should not have been afflicted by the common despair, an astonishing sloth was the rule. Activity became, in everyone's eyes, absurd, a futile effort without any compensation. Concern for the future seemed to be a sinister joke. Confronted with a choice between two tasks necessitating an equal effort, one of construction and the other of destruction, people generally opted, without remorse and even with a kind of lugubrious jubilation, for destruction.

Certain wilderness regions remained opulent and adorned, but wherever human still lived, the rich gardens and harmonious parks were sadly pillaged. To collect fruit, trees were felled; people set fire to forests to dissipate numbness in their fingers or without any apparent reason at all, lighting a fire being at least as natural as putting one out. The last vestiges of scientific civilization disappeared. The houses that were still intact remained open, and only sheltered temporary gusts; reserves were squandered; domestic animals wandered loose, searching in vain for some master.

Rapid means of communication soon ceased to exist entirely; sliders, aircraft, wheeled vehicles and ships of every sort—many of which were, in any case, unusable since the disappearance of the zones, were abandoned or destroyed. All that remained, here and there, were carts pulled by animals and slow sailing-gliders dangerous to use.

The Earth became free again, vast and wild.

Defeated humankind, condemned to death, agonized in sadness and ugliness.

Ordinarily, everyone lived in isolation. The last families broke up; the last remaining children, even the very young or infirm, were frequently abandoned by their parents. Ephemeral groups sometimes formed, but they were people in despair, coming together in order to die, or sick people driven by a diabolical instinct to gather together and travel in order to infect others.

It often happened that the concern for individual self-preservation lost its force. There were numerous suicides, and more numerous still were those who dragged themselves around, miserably, in a cowardly fashion, incapable of ensuring their own subsistence in the most prosperous environment.

Intelligence degenerated. Ideas were flat, dull and confused. A kind of bewilderment was observable in everyone, a homogeneous imbecility, sometimes accompanied by occasional crises of disordered effervescence. These crises were often confined to the insane. Among the less disequilibrated, they always constituted a morbid state, a feverish revolt, the last flicker of a flame on the point of going out. That momentary and abnormal mental activity was ordinarily manifest in a malevolent fashion; the excited individuals drew up plans of destruction, striving to discover methods of efficacious and rapid vandalism.

A few scientists tried, from time to time, to get back on their feet and search for a remedy that might bring salvation. The idea of an inconceivable, miraculous success, sustained them then, and they were almost happy, but most of them could not retain that attitude for long; after a few days, they abandoned everything.

Among the humble, that intermittent faith in a miracle appeared more rarely. On occasion however, a group welcomed some false news bearing an astonishing hope; there was a moment of joy, a brief revivification—then doubt returned, very quickly, and the group often fell apart before the truth was formally confirmed, everyone plunging more profoundly into isolation and distress.

Morality was no longer anything but a word designating indifferent habits. In that regard, humans descended below the level of any animate creature. The most ordinary and most facile virtues were also the rarest. A certain nonchalant heroism could still be encountered quite easily, but sincerity, respect for promises given and the most elementary gratitude were only manifest at increasingly rare intervals, and purely by hazard. The just seemed no longer to be distinguishable from the unjust. Al actions carried the same weight.

And all masks fell...

Especially at the times when individuals emerged from their habitual sluggishness, destructive sentiments were given free rein. Lies, treasons and hatreds were cynically unveiled. In the very bosom of the exceedingly rare families that had escaped the disaster, the ties of love were broken; ferocious antipathies or monstrous attractions, previously forcefully repressed, came to light.

The genetic instinct, exasperated, was subject to frightful perversions. Everywhere that survivors remained numerous, the sin of lust became feverish. There was no modesty, no restraint, no disgust, but a hideous and dismal confusion of sexes, ages and species. Couples formed at hazard for sordid encounters. Rape followed by murder was frequent; children fled in terror from brutes with human faces.

The men were abominable but the women were worse. They arrived sooner or later at a sanguinary frenzy, fits of veritable rage. The exhilarant vice exercised terrible ravages upon them, and often, in the silence of the night, lamentable laughter was heard, nostalgic appeals and hoarse cries of an infinite sadness, by which they lent themselves mutually to desperate embraces. Sometimes, grouped in bands, they tracked isolated males, striking and mutilating them with exceptional cruelty. Almost all of them openly indulged in bestiality. From time to time, they simulated pregnancy; half-demented, they deceived themselves and sometimes succeeded in persuading others. People followed them then and surrounded them with imperious concern, adoring their savior loins—until they day when the deception was discovered and they were ferociously beaten.

As the seasons succeeded one another, over the entire Earth, the number of human beings diminished rapidly, and the survivors, who were approaching the fatal terminus, sank into the most frightful melancholy and the vilest debauchery.

The continents were unaware of one another. There were only insignificant exchanges between regions, the slow migrations of the sick and the travels of the restless, roaming randomly along the easiest paths.

One summer evening, in the territory of Europe, three crazed female debauchees, who had been hunting a young boy all day, stopped on the edge of a forest, stupefied.

A couple emerged from the cover of the trees. The dark-skinned man, vigorous and tall, seemed hardly out of adolescence; the woman, even younger, perfectly beautiful with a cheerful face, was breast-feeding a tiny baby.

When the debauchees had recovered from their surprise, they launched themselves toward the magical apparition with one accord—but the couple had already fled, with the surprising agility of wild beasts, and two huge wild dogs, which had surged out of a thicket, barred the route, fangs threatening, ready to fight.

II. The Odyssey of Samuel and Flore

Samuel and Flore had stayed in the isolation chamber at the back of the vandalized laboratory for two days and nights. When hunger, thirst and the odor of the cadavers had obliged them to come out, the evolution of system 13 had concluded.

They went into the house, ate and drank. Sated, they recovered a little gaiety; they leapt about, chasing one another and laughing.

The silence made them anxious, however. Neither Harrisson, nor Lygie, nor Salem was there. They searched the house, calling out, faintly at first, and then with all their might, their voices trembling with anguish. In the courtyard they walked around the corpses without recognizing Salem's. In order to find Lygie they headed for the laboratory, but as soon as they reached the entrance to the vestibule a horrible odor caused them to retreat hurriedly. Fear gripped them again and they ran down the hill as far as their legs would carry them. They stopped, out of breath, in a little copse and went to sleep in one another's arms, huddled in tall ferns.

When the cold of the night woke them up, they called for their masters again. In the morning, slowly and prudently, sliding through the log grass from tree to tree, they returned to *The Refuge*, whether they appeased their hunger. Then they searched for Harrisson and Lygie again. The odor of the corpses made their nostrils quiver and their hair bristle. At dusk, they went back to the plain, running as far as a new shelter.

For an entire week they continued that routine. They were sad, not knowing which way to turn, and almost ill; only the pleasure of nourishment animated their gestures slightly.

Abundant fruits were scattered over the ground. On the eighth day, the two children gathered acorns of a delicate species and enormous beech-nuts. Recovering their self-possession at dawn, they started playing, in the morning light, with more enthusiasm than usual; then they started walking across the plain, randomly.

They next day, they retraced their steps; once again they climbed up to their former dwelling. A slow, heavy wind was carrying waves of pestilence. Flocks of crows were circling and plunging down with youthful cries. Two packs of dogs were fighting over a heap of bones. Even so, Samuel and Flore slipped into the house. The food-supplies had been devoured. By way of compensation, Flore found one of her dolls, which she took in her arms; for his part, Samuel discovered a knife and his favorite toy, a fire-wheel specially fabricated for him to Harrisson's design.

As the two children were still searching for something to eat, a big thin dog appeared, its eyes aflame, in a doorway. With one bound, Samuel and Flore reached the exit and ran away without looking back.

This time, they went a long way, crossing a river over a half-demolished bridge and not stopping until their strength gave out, beneath an oak-tree whose branches were weighed down by fruits. The trunk of the oak was hollow, forming a sort of little grotto. The two children huddled together inside it for the night. The next morning, they only had to reach out their arms to pick the exquisite acorns, very starchy and sweet.

When they had eaten, Flora cradled the doll and Samuel ignited some dry branches with his fire-wheel.

Then they thought about going back, but could not find the bridge over which they had passed the previous day.

The day was clear and mild; a little waterfall was singing. Flore stated to sing too, and Samuel skimmed stones over the water. They ate and drank again. Then, with their arms around one another's waist, they walked toward the sun, which was rising over the rounded edge of the Earth.

Every morning, they departed in the same fashion, in the direction of the greatest light.

They missed the caresses of their masters cruelly. Often, they were sad because of their solitude.

Furtively, they went through an unknown world full of ambushes. A blind man that they approached, thinking that they had recognized him as old Salem, spoke to them in an utterly terrifying voice and threw stones in their direction. Another time, when they had found provisions in an abandoned house, a dog had attacked Samuel and bitten him.

After these adventures, they avoided houses, roads, people and large menacing beasts. For preference, they moved in close proximity to cover, on paths that were scarcely cleared.

For some time they followed a wooded valley through which a wide river ran, and arrived in a region where people were still fairly numerous; they encountered several of them, who seemed very sad and malevolent. Gripped by fear, they fled, and went over the river by means of an intact bridge. In the days that followed, as they drew away from the valley, they fell upon an immense charnel-house. The odor chased them away. Walking toward the midday sun, they arrived on high ground where cheerful streams ran. The region was deserted, strewn with already-whitened bones. They stayed there for some time and their melancholy dissipated.

All around, the marvelous fruits of autumn weighed down the branches. Heavy rains fell, and then there was the caress of the sun again. Mushrooms pierced the verdure, as odorous as flowers. The domestic animals that had escaped the disaster were living freely; chickens were laying eggs under bushes. Samuel and Flore obtained their subsistence without any difficulty.

There was joy in their hearts.

All day long they played and danced.

Flore, cradling her doll, made long rhythmic speeches to it. With his wheel, Samuel set fire to dry twigs and resinous branches, and the both crouched over the tumultuous flower of fire.

At nightfall, they found shelter in brushwood or took refuge in the hollow trunk of some giant tree. Small carnivores were roaming around, which ran away at the slightest movement. Dogs often came to sniff the two children—thin, bold dogs whose eyes lit up in the darkness in the presence of that living flesh. Samuel and Flore, who had keen ears and slept lightly, stood up fearfully then. Usually, the dogs retreated, growling. Sometimes, on the contrary, they came with humble spines to lie down at the feet of the trembling vertical creatures. The two children refused the alliance, though; they climbed trees, and when daylight came, they chased the dogs away with voices and gestures.

Their intelligence developed slowly. The rudimentary language they had obtained from their masters was further simplified, and they remained incapable of true reasoning. They made certain very useful comparisons, however. Necessity rendered them ingenious and dexterous. As their clothes were turning to shreds and were no longer sufficient to protect them against the nocturnal cold, they collected others, warm and light furs that were lying in the vicinity of destroyed houses. At first, Samuel's wheel had only served for their amusement, but he learned gradually to make use of the virtues of fire. Flame was their friend, which reanimated their numb limbs and gave fruits a new savor. Creating fire and nourishing it became one of their principal preoccupations. The often did without the lighter-wheel. Harrisson, while he studied their behavior, had taught them to make fire with stones and certain dry branches, and Samuel had become astonishingly skillful at that game.

The first chills of winter surprised them in the region of high ground. A blistering wind chased them away, as well as numerous animals, in the direction of the midday sun, but high mountains barred their route; the earth was more arid, the fruits much scarcer. The two children were obliged to hunt small animals. They suffered, and their strength, instead of increasing, declined. For several days they were lost in the middle of an immense field of snow. The sun no longer appeared; their numb and awkward hands did not succeed in extracting fire from icy branches. They shivered in spite of their furs and were hungry. Fortunately, they found a little grotto in the depths of which they slept for a long time, tightly entwined.

When they left the grotto, thin and languid, mild gusts caressed their faces; winter was losing its grip. They went into a valley where rodents were swarming; without too much trouble they trapped a considerable number and ate avidly. Then they resumed their much toward warmer climes.

They walked through soft landscapes, and the generous season brought back joy. Their limbs had recovered their suppleness and an increased strength; their blood ran briskly.

They encountered more mountains, crossed rivers, and followed the beautiful shores of the sea for some while.

Winter came back, but not the cruel snow; the bounty of the sun remained spread over the earth.

They lived idly. It was not a taste for adventure that made them travel, nor the attraction of unknown horizons. They were obeying the obscure will of the earth and sky; they were obeying the sun, the clouds, the winds and the seasons. Above all, they were fleeing human beings. Several times they had been threatened and pursued, so they traversed inhabited regions, even the most hospitable, as rapidly as possible, On the other hand, they willingly lingered in deserted areas.

Their senses, naturally highly-developed, gradually acquired a singular acuity. They could see and hear at long distances, and their sense of smell recognized subtle effluvia as they passed. They allowed themselves to be surprised with increasing infrequency; as soon as they suspected the presence of human beings, they made off, nimbly and silently.

Their prudence was extreme; their courage, on every occasion, rather weak. Even in Samuel, at moments of danger, the bellicose instinct did not awaken.

Large herbivores excited their suspicion. They sometimes encountered herds of horses and ruminants wandering from one pasture to another, and often, some old animal, recovering its domestic habits before the human couple, came running in quest of an order to a caress. Immediately, however, the two children made themselves scarce.

After humans, they were most afraid of dogs. Their troubling packs were, in fact, beginning to roam the plains, where they indulged in violent combats. They could be seen passing in a whirlwind, their eyes on fire, mounting a derisory guard near old houses emptied of their inhabitants. Yet others, their gazes full of distress, howled plaintively and wandering in search of their masters.

One morning, Samuel and Flore, who had sent the night under a dense thorn-bush, found a large somber spaniel lying at their feet. They stood up abruptly and ran away at top speed. The dog followed them. While running, they threw stones at it and the dog stopped, looking sat them with its beautiful sad eyes. The next day, when they awoke, it was there again. For several days it accompanied them thus, at a distance, sometimes visible and sometimes invisible.

Full of anxiety at first, they eventually became slightly reassured and relenting their flight. One morning, they became bold enough to hit the dog. Then it lay down very close to them, stretching out on the ground, offering itself to blows with a tremor of joy. Then it departed like an arrow and disappeared into the shadow of a nearby thicket. It soon came back, carrying a hare in its jaws, still warm, which it deposited at Samuel's feet. The two children were hungry; they ate the hare, and when they had eaten it, they danced and wrestled. The dog dared not join in with their capers, but it leapt up and down on the spot, uttering faint joyful yaps.

In the days that followed, it brought them more game. The children were no longer afraid of it, and lived in abundance. Nevertheless, they remained distant, ready to break the pact.

One evening, the dog was late reappearing. They were hungry, and went to sleep full of sadness. The dog did not arrive until the following morning. It brought a bird of considerable size, but it had been fighting. Black blood was sticking the fur of its ears and throat together. Then Samuel and Flore fetched fresh water in the hollows of their hands and poured it over the wounds—and from that day on, the alliance was complete.

The new companion soon became accustomed to the name Ouaf.

Life became more cheerful and, at the same time, easier and more secure. The travelers slowly made their way through regions that were almost completely uninhabited. They spent long placid days beneath and clear and clement sky.

Samuel and Flore still fled from humans and animals that were intimidating by virtue of their size, but the alliance with the dog had widened. Ouaf now had a prosperous and rapidly growing family. There was Bow, the mother, a large brown beast with a heavy jaw, always on the alert and always ready for combat, and then the tribe of young ones, turbulent and variegated, hunters like Ouaf or as brave as Bow. When they passed by, carnivores hid; even the largest herbivores assembled their young and moved away.

One day, at the edge of an era in which a few humans still lived, two of the latter, who seemed prey to a furious dementia, pursued Flore. In spite of the rapidity of her pace, they were undoubtedly about to catch up with her when Bow arrived like a thunderbolt, with several of her aggressive sons behind her. The two men fell to the ground their throats slashed. Flore fled with Ouaf and the other dogs and Samuel brought the group after them with long strides.

Samuel had never had the idea of fighting...

Every season found him taller and stronger, but he remained gentle, prudent and furtive. When the guard-dogs raised the alarm, he started running, drawing Flore behind him. When he set off, if nothing hindered his surge, his velocity was equal to that of the most agile dogs. His long, lithe legs knew no fatigue, and the breath of his lungs seemed inexhaustible.

At the same time, Flore had blossomed to. Tall, with a flexible figure, she had tapering hips and round, fleshy limbs. Her voice was more ample, full of warm sonority.

One summer evening, after long days of abundance and idleness, as they were playing before going to sleep, Samuel, suddenly animate by an unfamiliar fury, his chest heaving, maintained his companion beneath him. And Flore, with her throat swollen, her eyes full of an anguished delight, uttered a long tremulous cry beneath the first stars.

They became more indolent, less avid for play, hunting and wrestling. Their affection for the dogs cooled temporarily. They no longer treated their allies on a equal footing. The dogs nourished them; they accepted the offerings but remained economical with caresses and refused to gambol with Bow's young sons.

Flore's gestures became harmonious and slow. Crowned with flowers, she pored over the water of springs. Often, she hid in the trees and Samuel, immediately anxious, called out to her. Then she allowed herself to be seen; swaying her polished torso, she advanced with small steps, gliding, rolling her hips, with her arms rounded above her head. Samuel bounded toward her and laid her down.

At the end of summer, there was an alarm; traveling humans were glimpsed in the vicinity. It was necessary to flee, quickly and for a long time. The ardor of their blood eased. Gradually, Flore became heavier; then her loins palpitated, and she refused the games of love completely.

The child uttered its first cry one evening at the renaissance of spring, in the depths of a grotto carpeted with dry grass. Flore drew the child to her breast and went to sleep, exhausted.

In the morning, while she was still asleep, Samuel picked up the child and silently took it out into the sunlight. Crouching down, he examined it curiously, and called to Ouaf. The dog came running, then Bow; soon, the entire tribe formed a circle around that whimpering ball of flesh. Bow was the first to understand that this was the beginning of a human being. She crouched down next to it and sniffed the pink limbs; then, with rapid little thrusts, she began licking it. Before that unusual spectacle, the entire tribe gave voice.

Then a cry of despair and fury resounded in the grotto. Alost immediately, Flore surged from the entrance and bounded into the middle of the group. Bow rolled on to her back, toppled by a kick. Samuel retreated precipitately, his face scratched.

Flore had picked up her child again. She raised it into the light and considered it. Then she advanced one of the dolorous points of her bosom toward the little pink mouth. Milk spurted out; the little lips adapted themselves to the proffered flesh.

Then Flore, appeased, smiled at the tribe of dogs sitting around her; and she also smiled at the bewildered Samuel, who used the back of his hand to wipe the blood from his slashed cheek.

The child immediately became the radiant center of the tribe; in him beat the heart of them all. Flore no longer played except with him. Samuel handled him with delicacy. The dogs were his slaves; as soon as he had the strength to roll over on the ground, they competed to get close to him. They deposited their most precious offerings within his reach. Bow, the terrible mother, whom Samuel and Ouaf only approached with precaution during the first days of suckling, confided her new-borns to the child.

The prudence of the guides increased further. Samuel climbed trees to scrutinize the horizon; Ouaf, raising his muzzle, interrogated the subtlest passing effluvia.

The tribe no longer had any fear of large herbivores, but still dreaded humans.

For a long time, humans were never sighted, so the vigilance of the watchers eventually diminished. And on one summer evening, when the air was heavy with powerful forest odors, Flore suddenly allowed herself to be taken by surprise suckling her infant.

There was a hectic flight into the thick shade of the forest. The following day, there was no new alert, but when dawn returned for the second time, Ouaf signaled humans in all directions.

Flore having hidden the child in the folds of her furs, the entire tribe moved off hastily. Soon, a group of humans came in view, blocking the path they were following. Flore recognized the women who had surprised her; behind the women were two white men mounted on horses. One of the men, perceiving the tribe, cried out; his raised hand released a vivid fire and the sound of thunder.

Samuel was already retreating, but, in response to the white man's signal, other noises replied, along with cries and appeals. The danger was approaching from all sides at the same time. Surrounded, the tribe assembled around Flore. In the lead, Bow, her fur bristling, advanced slowly; then came all her heavy-jawed sons, then the human couple, the younger dog, the long-nosed hunters, and finally Ouaf, holding his head high.

Suddenly, Bow charged, and behind her, with a terrible surge, the wild band of combatants. The three women did not have time to turn and flee; they fell, and the howling of the dogs drowned out the screams of their brief death-throes. With a formidable leap, the boldest of Bow's sons had thrown himself at the first horseman; the man, unseated, had scarcely touched the ground before Bow tore out his throat. The other ran away, as fast as his horse could carry him.

The way was clear. Samuel, Flore and the hunters raced forward. A detonation increased their fear and the rapidity of their flight. They reached a thicket and plunged into it.

Bow and the combatants returned to the tribe shortly afterwards, their fangs still bloody. Ouaf was missing, struck from behind by an invisible hand wielding thunder. Bow retraced her steps; having found the cadaver, she sniffed it for a long time, and then howled until nightfall. When she rejoined her family, she was unapproachable for several hours.

The pursuit had ceased. No one among the enemy had seen the child.

The tribe, however, continued to flee, seeking deserted territory. They only paused after a very long journey, on a grassy plateau. There was a drought, and they were short of water. The absence of Ouaf, the incomparable hunter, made itself cruelly felt. The tribe suffered.

It was in that place that Samuel learned to fight. One day, he was with Flore under a tree in the middle of the empty plateau; not far away, the child was crawling in the long grass. They were alone with the newborn dogs, for in that time of famine all the adults were in pursuit of the scarce game. Samuel and Flore were thin, weary and somnolent. They did not notice two flying men who were moving silently at low altitude in slow gliders.

The two men suddenly stopped and landed near the tree under which the couple was lying. Then they ran toward the child and grabbed him. Wonderstruck, they lifted the little body above their heads and their joy burst forth in loud exclamations. Flore and Samuel stood up. With a roar, the mother launched herself toward the strangers. Samuel had already started to run away, but a shrill cry from the baby stopped him. He came back, breaking off a heavy branch as he came, and with astonishing rapidity he killed...

When the two men were motionless at his feet, he remained momentarily bewildered, his entire body trembling. Then he circled around the cadavers, gradually drawing away from them, until Bow and the other hunters returned. When the tribe was reassembled he stopped trembling, and gamboled with the dogs.

The following night, the rain fell abundantly. The members of the tribe, their thirst quenched, resumed their march. Samuel took the lead, preceding Bow, carrying a massive club. He soon exchanged the club for a heavy metal hammer that he found along the way. In his hands it was a terrible weapon, which he was not to abandon again while his strength lasted.

The tribe passed through a region that was not completely uninhabited. Several times, they were unable to avid isolated human beings. If surprised while alone or with the dogs, Samuel fled, but if Flore was with him, he charged without hesitation and struck mortally. His authority over the dogs increased; the leader of the hunt, he imposed discipline on Bow's most turbulent sons and led them against the large herbivores.

When summer returned, the tribe lived tranquilly on the slope of a high mountain. The terrain was difficult at first but rich in game, and no trace of living humans was ever found there. Water ran in limpid streams; caves offered reliable shelters. Fruit trees of all species covered the slopes. On the lower ground plants bearing dry grains grew abundantly, almost as nourishing as the flesh of herbivores. There was, in addition, no lack of the latter on the mountain and in the valley. They lived there in numerous bands, and were almost harmless. There was Moûh the ox, Ouhin the horse, Horoho the pig, Bêê the warm fur, and others.

Flore gave birth. She had two daughters, so similar that only the mother could tell them apart. She named them Hâ and Hahâ; the firstborn, who laughed a great deal, had already received the name Bihihi.

Shortly after the birth of the twins, flying humans passed over in gliders carried into the valley by the wind. The young dogs imprudently barked a threat at them, but Flore had hidden with her children and the sad passengers did not discover the mountain's marvelous secret.

Flore no longer joined in with voyages of exploration or hunting. She never risked her family away from cover. Under the guard of a few dogs, she remained in the cave; she nourished the fire, bandaged the injured and taught her children songs and games.

On the side of the mountain she gave birth several times. She had Nouhou, a male, then two daughters, Voho and Ruhi. About the time of Ruhi's birth, Samuel imposed on the aging Bow an alliance with Ouhin the horse—and Samuel led the hunt rapidly, over long distances.

One day, he happened to penetrate into a narrow valley where a pack of wolf-dogs was pursuing Horoho the black. Mounted on Ouhin, Samuel attacked the wolf-dogs with his hammer; there was a terrible battle. The tribe was victorious, but not without dolorous losses. Bow perished, along with several of her most ardent sons.

The wolf-dogs followed their vanquishers at a distance, and the next day, their menacing howls were heard at the foot of the mountain. They settled in the valley, thus barring the hunting route. Numerous, patient and full of hatred, they laid siege to the tribe, attacking any isolated individual. Distant expeditions became impossible. After the arrival of the wolf-dogs, the region became depopulated. Horoho could no longer be found; Mouh left for other pastures, his redoubtable males protecting the young.

The starving tribe came down the mountain, and fought their way out. Ouhin carried the children and they made rapid progress, but the wolf-dogs still followed. It was necessary to defend themselves again by fighting, and anyone who strayed from the group did not come back. Imprudent fury caused the death of more than one of Bow's sons.

Samuel tried to think of ruses.

He drew the enemy into a vast grassland, and when the wind was blowing away from the tribe he started fires in several places. The wind gave birth to innumerable red flowers and drove them to the edge of the horizon. Eating all the grass of the savannah, the fire finally chased the wolf-dogs away.

The region was not safe, though. The tribe wandered for a long time. Several times, they were obliged to hide in order to avoid the gaze of flying men. They went around a vast territory in which fire had devoured everything. Isolated humans on foot, whom the dogs' scent had not been able to indentify, and with whom they suddenly found themselves confronted, were killed. Such encounters became increasingly rare, and they soon ceased to see flying humans.

The tribe arrived in an immense wooded plain; no humans were living there. They stopped there.

Samuel had reached the full development of his strength. Flore gave birth at regular intervals. Hâ, Hahâ and their younger sisters also began, in their turn, to produce sons and daughters. Then Flore no longer gave birth.

Bihihi had surpassed Samuel in strength and speed. Having received the hammer of command from his father's hands, he became the leader of the hunt.

Nouhou, by contrast, wounded in his youth in a combat against Moûh, took no part in major expeditions, but he was full of patience and cunning. He made an alliance with his old enemy Moûh, and then with Bêê of the precious fur, and he was also able to attract Horoho, who was domesticated.

Nouhou gave names to beings and things. He knew better than the women how to charm children with continuous rhythmic cries—and on mild summer evenings, when the most beautiful of the maidens led the round-dance of their nubile sisters among the vaporous pallors of the moon, Nouhou accompanied the dance of love with a slow and voluptuous song.

III. The Song of the Morning

The tribe slept in a vast grotto whose rocky opening overlooked the plain.

The leader of the hunt, Eléoum, son of Oréa, who was the son of Ruhi, got up from his bed of dry leaves and came to the entrance of the cave. The watchers gave voice; the tribe woke up.

The women having nourished the fire, the hunters approached the large hearths whose flames awoke the strength of their limbs.

Eléoum uttered a long cry of summons. In the neighboring thickets, Horoho grunted, muzzle to the ground, and Moûh snorted idly without moving, but Ouhin came running immediately.

The tribe ate. Young dogs squabbled; bones cracked between their teeth.

Finally, the sun darted long arrows at ground level. Old Nouhou advanced on to the platform of rocks; maidens followed him, crowned with foliage. The tribe fell silent. Nouhou sang, his hands turned toward the star; the rhythm of his voice led the harmonious gestures of the maidens.

When Nouhou fell silent, the tribe uttered its cry.

Eléoum descended into the plain, guiding the first hunters. Ouhin carried the men. There were only young males there, as strong and sprightly as fire. They were more numerous than the fingers of two hands. And for each man there were three dogs: two short-ears, chosen from among the boldest combatants, and one long-nose, skilled at following the tenuous thread of odors attached to the grass.

At a gesture from Eléoum, the hunters deployed in a line. The long-noses took the lead. Birds took flight, rodents made off, and Horoho the black and the large wild herbivores soon got up. The long-noses saluted their flight with brief barking, but did not chase after them with their usual joyful ardor, for Eléoum and the first hunters were not pursuing the furtive game necessary to the tribe.

Eléoum was hunting for dry humans...

Since the distant time when Bihihi had taken the chief's red hammer, the tribe had lived placidly. Strong by virtue of the courage of the dogs and the cunning of Flore's sons, it had triumphed without difficulty in its encounters with vagabond carnivores. Hardly suffering at all, it had lived idly, without undertaking long journeys.

Samuel had died, and then Flore; in his turn, Bihihi had handed on the hammer of command. And the slow seasons had gone by, full of sunlight or cold, and the changing moon had glided through night after night beneath the blinking eyes of the stars, without the vertical creature dreaded by the ancients of the tribe ever having been seen.

Then, one day, a child who had strayed from the grotto disappeared. Oréa, the leader of the hunt, had set out to look for it. A long-nose, following the trail, soon arrived in a wood where two very old men whose flesh had been melted by time were caressing the child gently and weeping with joy.

Oréa was alone with the long-nose and had never fought beings of his own race. He was afraid, and went back to the tribe. The cries of the women rose up against him; the anguished males did not budge.

Then Eléoum, the young son with blazing eyes whose turbulence had already made the tribe anxious more than once, stood up among the hunters. He went after the old men in the wood and killed them. When he had deposited the child on the threshold of the grotto, he took the hammer of command from the hands of his father Oréa.

The following day, more humans were scented. The old ones wanted to flee, but Eléoum, assembling the less fearful males, led them against the strangers.

The hunt had being going on for two moons. For two moons, in that region where the tribe had lived secretly for so long, humans had been arriving from all points of the horizon.

There were dried-up men, older than Bihihi, and women more decrepit than Hahâ. They came slowly, isolated or in little groups, sometimes with dogs. They came painfully—and yet, nothing stopped them! A mysterious will seemed to be guiding their steps in the direction of the tribe. They were marching toward the goal of their life.

The first ones that Eléoum attacked did not defend themselves; nor did they try to run away; they died with ecstatic eyes. Later, some came whose attitude was, on the contrary, haggard and ferocious. Full of cunning, they sometimes succeeded in eluding the dogs. A few, bearing light weapons that nevertheless had a cruel bite, engaged in battle, fighting desperately until the end. One woman who created the terrible thunderous fire at the ends of her arms decimated Eléoum's troop before being killed.

Then the encounters became less frequent and less dangerous. Since the end of the first moon, the hunters had only struck down strangers as inoffensive as Moûh the young or even Bêê.

Now, the passage of dry humans seemed to have come to a end. Three times now, Eléoum had gone forth as far as the distant boundary of the sky without seeing any.

This hunt would be the last before the festivals of summer and love, for, after slow rains, the season of luminous joy would return, and the tribe would recover its ardor of life...

The fleeing birds and quadrupeds passed out of range of the scouts. Suddenly, there was a raucous barking. The line of dogs wavered, the men shivered. A young long-nose followed an odorous trail, but lost it almost immediately. The other scouts, having rallied, found noting there but the heavy effluvia of a herd of herbivores. They corrected the young fool who had been thus deceived and recovered their positions.

The hunters marched until sunset. On the edge of a wood they built a fire, and the flesh of a large herbivore appeased their hunger. Then they went to sleep under the trees.

Before dawn they got up, full of anxiety; the watchers had scented dry humans!

Fury illuminated Eléoum's eyes and caused his heart to sing. Mounted on Ouhin, he led his troop at great speed behind the long-noses, who, following a straight trail, bounded forwards, sure of their route.

At daybreak, the enemy was in sight. The vertical creature advanced slowly; like all the others, she was walking toward the distant tribe. She was not alone; a strong clan of wild dogs accompanied her.

The hunters hesitated, but Eléoum whirled the red hammer, and they all surged forward, howling. The vertical creature had stopped; her dogs formed up, ready to pounce, their necks extended, swollen by furious barking.

The first impact was terrible; almost all the dogs rolled on the ground. The short-ears, less numerous, were coming off worse, but Ouhin came to their rescue and the clubs of the men broke the animals' jaws.

Eléoum had headed straight for the principal enemy. It was a woman, older than the oldest of his tribe. Tangled white hair fell down her thin back, and there was no flesh on the bones of her limbs. She seemed devoid of strength, but her eyes were frightful. Eléoum had fought humans and the most ferocious beasts but none had every looked at him with a similar gaze and he had never seen a grimace comparable to the rictus of that toothless mouth.

The woman was carrying a shiny weapon, long and frail. As she raised her arm, Eléoum dreaded the thunder-fire, but the fire did not emerge, and the hunter uttered his victory cry.

The woman fell, knocked over by Ouhin. Leaping to the ground, Eléoum was beside her with a single bound, his hammer raised. Upright on his long legs, he arched his back to deliver a forceful blow. Then, with a strange laugh, a kind of tremulous howl, the woman thrust her weapon between Eléoum's dark thighs, and with a single twist, rapid and sure, severed his virility. The hammer fell immediately, smashing the vile face.

With the woman dead, the wild dogs no longer resisted. The short-ears drove them back toward the edge of the sky. Then the troop of hunters took the road back to the grotto. In spite of the victory, the return was silent.

Seated on Ouhin and supported by two of his brothers, Eléoum, his head swaying, watched the blood flow from his thighs. The compress of leaves applied to his wound did not heal it. Cold gained his limbs; a mysterious breath snuffed out the blaze of his eyes. His hand had dropped the red hammer, and the hunters took turns to carry the chief's weapon. They were sad and almost fearful. Wounded dogs were dragging themselves along with difficulty.

When the rocky hill on whose flank the tribe lived finally appeared o the horizon, the vague anguish weighing upon the hunters was dissipated. Ouhin increased his pace; the youngest dogs began to gambol. Then the men uttered loud cries, and the watchers in the distance replied.

The sun had hidden in its inaccessible thickets at the far side of the plain. Around the grotto, flame-flowers were blooming, nourished by shadows. High flames twisted or lay down in the grip of the wind.

In the light of the fires, rapid silhouettes were passing back and forth, but the gestures thus designed to the eyes of the hunters did not have the nonchalance of dances or games. The tribe seemed to be prey to an unusual agitation.

At the foot of the hill, the hunters, anxious again, uttered their cry once again: "Eïa! Ha! Ha!"

Only the watchdogs replied. Then, forgetting their fatigue, those who had been traveling across the plain for two days launched themselves swiftly on to the rising path.

The entire tribe had formed a circle some distance from the principal hearth. Carrying Eléoum, the hunters came closer, but surprise suddenly nailed them to the spot. Kneeling on the ground beside the fire, Nouhou was supporting the head of a dry human lying on the ground.

The stranger had been discovered near the grotto when the sun was at its hottest. For long days he had been marching toward the tribe. Mingling his trail with that of the herbivores, he had deceived the dogs; the day before, even the first hunters, despite being warned by the brief anxiety of the young log-nose, had drawn away, leaving him behind them. And the man, with a supreme effort, had climbed the hill. He had been found in a thicket, lying next to Moûh, unable to speak. Because he seemed inanimate, the dogs had not attacked him. Nouhou had come with the women and the youngest hunters. The stranger was lying there; he was a man with white skin, very old; his feet were bleeding; his knees and hands had similarly been torn by stones and brushwood.

After a few moments, when he opened his eyes, Nouhou, approaching cautiously, had deposited a shell full of Moûh's milk within the reach of his arm—for Nouhou, an enemy of combats, thought of making an alliance with the dry human, as he had done with Moûh, Bêê and Horoho.

Having drunk the milk, the man had extended his hands toward the women and the young hunters.

That is why Nouhou was now supporting the dry man's head; he was asking the fire to awaken the strength of the poor torn body and, to facilitate the enchantment, he was repeating long, soft syllables in a monotonous voice.

Recovered from their surprise, the first hunters abruptly opened the circle and advanced, growling. Without interrupting himself, however, Nouhou gestured to them to go away. They also laid Eléoum down beside the fire and slipped the red hammer into his hand. Then they squatted down, silent and suspicious.

Nouhou deposited choice fruits next to the stranger, highly perfumed meat and warm furs. To seal the alliance definitively, he took a baby from the breast of a trembling woman and held it out to the dry man. The accursed one held out his feeble arms; his fingers caressed the infant, and he was transfigured by an incomparable joy. The tribe, anxious until then, breathed deeply.

The first hunters were still growling, though. Eléoum remained motionless and mute, and the frightful wound in his loins appeared to the eyes of the tribe. Women and old hunters, full of anxiety, cried: "Eléoum! Eléoum!"

Oréa, the father, advanced to the recumbent man's side, and called to him with all the strength of his voice: "Eléoum! Eléoum!"

The young chief was seen to emerge slowly from death. His vast chest swelled and he rose up on his wrists. He looked around, but his eyes remained dull and unfocused.

Suddenly, his entire body shivered. He had just perceived the dry man! It was as if the thunder-fire had penetrated his limbs. He uttered a roar, and leapt up. The red hammer smashed the breast of the dry man, whose bones broke.

Eléoum collapsed upon his victim. His loins had begun to bleed again; somersaults agitated his body, and then there was a tremor that did not stop. The dry man was choking, but his hands were still moving; his hands continued their caress on Eléoum's dark sides, and his pale face as illuminated by a supernatural happiness.

They both surrendered to death at the same time, when the moon, having arrived at the height of its course, began to slide down the slope of the sky.

Nouhou sang until dawn in a plaintive voice, and the hunters sang with him. The hunters were lamenting the death of Eléoum, but Nouhou was also regretting the stranger with the eyes full of tenderness in the radiant white face.

When Nouhou, guiding the maidens, went to salute the return of the sun, he carried the red hammer. He advanced to the edge of the platform and hurled the hammer into the brush at the foot of the hill. None of the hunters dared go down to look for it.

Nouhou was dead, thinking about the alliance so rapidly broken, and his eyes turned to the turbulent hunters.

He assembled Ouhin, two old long-noses full of cunning, and a few young men who were good singers and as gentle as maidens, and then he went down into the plain.

In his turn, he searched for dry humans. Neither he nor his companions was carrying a club, but in order to appease strangers and capture their confidence, they had fruits, delicate mushrooms, meat whose aroma had been brought out by the fire, and skillfully-woven crowns of foliage.

Slowly, they traveled the plain in every direction; they went as far as the edge of the sky, to the distant thickets neighboring the thickets of the sun—but the accursed race had vanished forever from that part of the Earth.

Nouhou was obliged to renounce the impossible amity.

His subsequent voyages were not as long. At the foot of the hill, he attempted to make an alliance with the birds, and imitated their songs.

Liberated from any threat, the tribe recovered its ingenuous gaiety. The disquieting flames in the eyes of the hunters were extinguished. The sound of voices was animated, but as soft as birdsong in the profound foliage, for the days of bright light had come...

The women made beautiful rounded gestures. The maidens with nimble feet ran into the thickets; their laughter, falling like light rain, troubled the nonchalant hunters.

Suddenly, the joy of the tribe blossomed like the swift flower of flame; the festivals of then sun and love began.

Old Nouhou directed the dances and songs.

Before dawn, when the weary couples lay down again, he came alone to the moon-blanched rocks, to offer the first hymn of the day to the allied or prowling beasts, to the whispering trees, to the plain asleep beneath the mist, and to the invisible and mysterious beings whose eyes were blinking between the moving clouds.

And in his voice trembled hope for times to come, innumerable days full of dazzling light and slow nights bathed by love.

Beneath the enormous quietude of the sky, he informed the pacified earth of the youthful hope of the idle, gentle, singing race.

SF & FANTASY

Henri Allorge. *The Great Cataclysm*
Guy d'Armen. *Doc Ardan: The City of Gold and Lepers*
G.-J. Arnaud. *The Ice Company*
Charles Asselineau. *The Double Life*
Cyprien Bérard. *The Vampire Lord Ruthwen*
Aloysius Bertrand. *Gaspard de la Nuit*
Richard Bessière. *The Gardens of the Apocalypse*
Albert Bleunard. *Ever Smaller*
Félix Bodin. *The Novel of the Future*
Alphonse Brown. *City of Glass*
André Caroff. *The Terror of Madame Atomos; Miss Atomos; The Return of Madame Atomos; The Mistake of Madame Atomos; The Monsters of Madame Atomos; The Revenge of Madame Atomos*
Félicien Champsaur. *The Human Arrow; Ouha*
Didier de Chousy. *Ignis*
Captain Danrit. *Undersea Odyssey*
C. I. Defontenay. *Star (Psi Cassiopeia)*
Charles Derennes. *The People of the Pole*
Georges Dodds (anthologist). *The Missing Link*
Harry Dickson. *The Heir of Dracula*
Jules Dornay. *Lord Ruthven Begins*
Alfred Driou. *The Adventures of a Parisian Aeronaut*
Sâr Dubnotal *vs. Jack the Ripper*
Alexandre Dumas. *The Return of Lord Ruthven*
Renée Dunan. *Baal*
J.-C. Dunyach. *The Night Orchid; The Thieves of Silence*
Henri Duvernois. *The Man Who Found Himself*
Achille Eyraud. *Voyage to Venus*
Henri Falk. *The Age of Lead*
Paul Féval. *Anne of the Isles; Knightshade; Revenants; Vampire City; The Vampire Countess; The Wandering Jew's Daughter*
Paul Féval, *fils. Felifax, the Tiger-Man*
Charles de Fieux. *Lamékis*
Arnould Galopin. *Doctor Omega*; *Doctor Omega & The Shadowmen*
G.L. Gick. *Harry Dickson and the Werewolf of Rutherford Grange*
Léon Gozlan. *The Vampire of the Val-de-Grâce*
Edmond Haraucourt. *Illusions of Immortality*
Nathalie Henneberg. *The Green Gods*

V. Hugo, P. Foucher & P. Meurice. *The Hunchback of Notre-Dame*
Michel Jeury. *Chronolysis*
Gustave Kahn. *The Tale of Gold and Silence*
Gérard Klein. *The Mote in Time's Eye*
Jean de La Hire. *Enter the Nyctalope; The Nyctalope on Mars; The Nyctalope vs. Lucifer; The Nyctalope Steps In; Night of the Nyctalope*
Etienne-Léon de Lamothe-Langon. *The Virgin Vampire*
André Laurie. *Spiridon*
Gabriel de Lautrec. *The Vengeance of the Oval Portrait*
Alain le Drimeur. *The Future City*
Georges Le Faure & Henri de Graffigny. *The Extraordinary Adventures of a Russian Scientist Across the Solar System* (2 vols.)
Gustave Le Rouge. *The Vampires of Mars The Dominion of the World* (w/Gustave Guitton) (4 vols.)
Jules Lermina. *Mysteryville; Panic in Paris; To-Ho and the Gold Destroyers; The Secret of Zippelius*
Jean-Marc & Randy Lofficier. *Edgar Allan Poe on Mars; The Katrina Protocol; Pacifica; Robonocchio; Tales of the Shadowmen 1-8*
Xavier Mauméjean. *The League of Heroes*
Joseph Méry. *The Tower of Destiny*
Hippolyte Mettais. *The Year 5865*
Louise Michel. *The Human Microbes; The New World*
José Moselli. *Illa's End*
John-Antoine Nau. *Enemy Force*
Marie Nizet. *Captain Vampire*
C. Nodier, A. Beraud & Toussaint-Merle. *Frankenstein*
Henri de Parville. *An Inhabitant of the Planet Mars*
Gaston de Pawlowski. *Journey to the Land of the 4th Dimension*
Georges Pellerin. *The World in 2000 Years*
Ernest Pérochon. *The Frenetic People*
Pierre Pelot. *The Child Who Walked on the Sky*
J. Polidori, C. Nodier, E. Scribe. *Lord Ruthven the Vampire*
P.-A. Ponson du Terrail. *The Vampire and the Devil's Son*
Henri de Régnier. *A Surfeit of Mirrors*
Maurice Renard. *The Blue Peril; Doctor Lerne; The Doctored Man; A Man Among the Microbes; The Master of Light*
Jean Richepin. *The Wing*
Albert Robida. *The Adventures of Saturnin Farandoul; The Clock of the Centuries; Chalet in the Sky*

J.-H. Rosny Aîné. *Helgvor of the Blue River; The Givreuse Enigma; The Mysterious Force; The Navigators of Space; Vamireh; The World of the Variants; The Young Vampire*
Marcel Rouff. *Journey to the Inverted World*
Han Ryner. *The Superhumans*
Brian Stableford. *The New Faust at the Tragicomique; The Empire of the Necromancers (The Shadow of Frankenstein; Frankenstein and the Vampire Countess; Frankenstein in London); Sherlock Holmes & The Vampires of Eternity; The Stones of Camelot; The Wayward Muse.* (anthologist) *The Germans on Venus; News from the Moon; The Supreme Progress; The World Above the World; Nemoville; Investigations of the Future*
Jacques Spitz. *The Eye of Purgatory*
Kurt Steiner. *Ortog*
Eugène Thébault. *Radio-Terror*
C.-F. Tiphaigne de La Roche. *Amilec*
Théo Varlet. *The Xenobiotic Invasion; Timeslip Troopers* (w/André Blandin); *The Martian Epic* (w/Octave Joncquel)
Paul Vibert. *The Mysterious Fluid*
Villiers de l'Isle-Adam. *The Scaffold; The Vampire Soul*
Philippe Ward. *Artahe*
Philippe Ward & Sylvie Miller. *The Song of Montségur*

MYSTERIES & THRILLERS

M. Allain & P. Souvestre. *The Daughter of Fantômas*
A. Anicet-Bourgeois, Lucien Dabril. *Rocambole*
A. Bernède. *Belphegor; Judex* (w/Louis Feuillade)
A. Bisson & G. Livet. *Nick Carter vs. Fantômas*
V. Darlay & H. de Gorsse. *Lupin vs. Holmes: The Stage Play*
Paul Féval. *Gentlemen of the Night; John Devil; The Black Coats ('Salem Street; The Invisible Weapon; The Parisian Jungle; The Companions of the Treasure; Heart of Steel; The Cadet Gang; The Sword-Swallower)*
Emile Gaboriau. *Monsieur Lecoq*
Steve Leadley. *Sherlock Holmes: The Circle of Blood*
Maurice Leblanc. *Arsène Lupin vs. Countess Cagliostro; Lupin vs. Holmes (The Blonde Phantom; The Hollow Needle); The Many Faces of Arsène Lupin*
Gaston Leroux. *Chéri-Bibi; The Phantom of the Opera; Rouletabille & the Mystery of the Yellow Room*

Richard Marsh. *The Complete Adventures of Judith Lee*
William Patrick Maynard. *The Terror of Fu Manchu; The Destiny of Fu Manchu*
Frank J. Morlock. *Sherlock Holmes: The Grand Horizontals; Sherlock Holmes vs Jack the Ripper*
Antonin Reschal. *The Adventures of Miss Boston*
P. de Wattyne & Y. Walter. *Sherlock Holmes vs. Fantômas*
David White. *Fantômas in America*

SCREENPLAYS

Mike Baron. *The Iron Triangle*
Emma Bull & Will Shetterly. *Nightspeeder; War for the Oaks*
Gerry Conway & Roy Thomas. *Doc Dynamo*
Steve Englehart. *Majorca*
James Hudnall. *The Devastator*
Jean-Marc & Randy Lofficier. *Royal Flush*
J.-M. & R. Lofficier & Marc Agapit. *Despair*
J.-M. & R. Lofficier & Joël Houssin. *City*
Andrew Paquette. *Peripheral Vision*
Robert L. Robinson, Jr. *Judex*
R. Thomas, J. Hendler & L. Sprague de Camp. *Rivers of Time*

NON-FICTION

Stephen R. Bissette. *Blur 1-5. Green Mountain Cinema 1; Teen Angels*
Win Scott Eckert. *Crossovers* (2 vols.)
Jean-Marc & Randy Lofficier. *Shadowmen* (2 vols.)
Randy Lofficier. *Over Here*

HEXAGON COMICS

Franco Frescura & Luciano Bernasconi. *Wampus*
Franco Frescura & Giorgio Trevisan. *CLASH*
L. Bernasconi, J.-M. Lofficier & Juan Roncagliolo Berger. *Phenix*
Claude Legrand, J.-M. Lofficier & L. Bernasconi. *Kabur*
Franco Oneta. *Zembla*
L. Buffolente, Lofficier & J.-J. Dzialowski. *Strangers: Homicron*
Danilo Grossi. *Strangers: Jaydee*
Claude Legrand & Luciano Bernasconi. *Strangers: Starlock*

ART BOOKS

Jean-Pierre Normand. *Science Fiction Illustrations*
Raven Okeefe. *Raven's L'il Critters; Rave's Faves*
Randy Lofficier & Raven Okeefe. *If Your Possum Go Daylight...*
Daniele Serra. *Illusions*